D1255351

CHRIS KENISTON

USA TODAY BESTSELLING AUTHOR

Indie House Publishing

This book is a work of fiction. Names, characters, places and incidents are the product of the author's imagination or are used fictionally. Any resemblance to actual events, locales, or persons, living or dead, is coincidental.

Indie House Publishing

BOOKS BY CHRIS KENISTON

Aloha Series
Aloha Texas
Almost Paradise
Mai Tai Marriage
Dive Into You
Shell Game
Look of Love
Love by Design
Love Walks In
Waikiki Wedding

Surf's Up Flirts
(Aloha Series Companions)
Shall We Dance
Love on Tap
Head Over Heels
Perfect Match
Just One Kiss
It Had to Be You

Honeymoon Series
Honeymoon for One
Honeymoon for Three

Family Secrets Novels
Champagne Sisterhood
The Homecoming
Hope's Corner

Farraday Country

Adam

Brooks

Connor

Declan

Ethan

Finn

Grace

Hannah

Ian

ACKNOWLEDGEMENTS

Finn has been a fun book to write. I have to say, as the rancher of the family, Finn was the story I worried about the most. Without the help of a review team member, Katrena Crimm, I would never have had a clue about ranch dogs, moving cattle, or rattle snakes. Thank you, Katrena, for your patient responses to endless questions on everything ranching from livestock to fences.

As has grown to be a custom with anything dealing with horses, the books wouldn't work nearly so well without help from my good author friend, JM Madden. The woman writes great military romance and really knows her horses! Thank you.

In an effort to produce the Farraday books quickly, I have become very dependent on the support and encouragement of many friends. Author Kathy Ivan for allowing me to commandeer my own corner of her house. The Plotting Princesses for answering the call to stuck story lines. To Mary Sullivan for coming up with the right answers when I can't see the forest for the trees. And Cheryl Lucas for keeping my logistics straight. Y'all are the best!

As I mention often on my Facebook page #gottahavefriends!

Thanks for joining me with Finn.

Enjoy!
Chris

CHAPTER ONE

Four years at Texas A&M and Joanna Gaines had seen a lot of cow country. But not all the ranchland near College Station combined could compare to the vast nothingness called West Texas.

Pulled over at the side of the road, she'd taken a drink from the cooler and downed most of it in a single gulp. At the beginning of her trek from ghost town to town, she'd drink her favorite cola. Not long into this new adventure of hours between destination and the unforgiving Texas sun beating down on a person, she'd bought a cooler to keep in her trunk and stocked it with bottled water. Folding the marked up map in front of her and placing it in the glove compartment, she figured she had to be getting pretty close to Finn's.

In her breast pocket, her phone buzzed. *Linda.* "No, I haven't been eaten by a coyote. No, I haven't been bitten by a snake. And no, I have not been captured by Indians."

"I did not say a word about Indians," her sister huffed.

"But you did mention coyotes, snakes, and, I believe, mountain lions."

"It was bobcats."

"Oh yeah, forgive me." Joanna took another drink of water. "Bobcats. Right."

"You know, if you got a regular nine to five job in an office like normal people with a college degree, I wouldn't have to worry."

Joanna screwed the cap on the empty bottle and tossed it into the back seat. She was going to have to clean the thing out soon, her interior was beginning to look like a salvage yard. "You like worrying. It gives you purpose in life."

"I'd rather be adrift if it'll keep you within spitting distance of a real city."

"As opposed to a fake city." On the other side of the fence a few horses grazed in the distance. One in particular picked that moment to look up at her. The beautiful animal and her foal would make a stunning picture. "Listen, I need to get going, we can pick up on this old argument another day."

"And what about Peter?"

Camera strap in hand, Joanna blew out a sigh. "What about him?"

"He came by my office yesterday."

"Persistent little—"

"Joanna…"

"Look, I'm sorry, but one very boring dinner date does not a relationship make."

"I think he wants another chance."

She really wanted to take the photograph before the horses moved. "If he comes by again tell him I've joined the Peace Corps."

"Joanna."

"French Foreign Legion?" Camera strap over her shoulder, she slowly ducked between the taught fence wires to the same side as the horses and eased toward the only shade tree she'd seen for miles.

"I'm not going to lie."

She glanced back toward her car and the map she'd folded away and smiled. "Tell him I've come home to my husband."

••••

"Man that feels good." Finn set his hat by his side, leaned against the post, and lifted his face to the sun.

"Move went pretty quick this morning." Finn's dad, Sean Farraday, looked across the pasture at the contented cows, drinking and snacking and pretty much doing what cows do all year long.

"Mothering up went well, too."

"Yep." A couple of mother cows were still looking for their calf, but not as many had been separated en route to this pasture as in days past. So far, the few that seemed hellbent on going back where they came from were being held behind the invisible line in the grass the dogs had drawn. Scratching the dust from his hair, Finn put his hat back on and listened to the steady thrum of cows calling out for their calves, or perhaps simply chewing the fat with their friends.

The best part of saddling up in the pitch black of early morning to start moving cows at first light was the chance to relax and watch Mother Nature at work until lunchtime. "Flow seems off on the water. I'll pull the pump tomorrow before we start working on the new fence section."

Sean nodded and sat beside his son. "Some days, I look out at the pasture and I'd swear I can see you and your brothers roping the dummy, or playing with the water, or even just worn out and napping."

A smile took over Finn's face. He remembered those days well. Especially when they wound up in pastures by the creek. Those were fun times swimming, catching toads, and all around doing his best to keep up with his older brothers.

"Gates closed. So far none of the herd is backtracking." Sam, their ranch hand, left his horse ground-tied with the others and came up beside his bosses. "Are we taking turns heading back to the house for lunch?"

Shaking his head, Finn pulled a blade of grass from the ground. "Nope. Aunt Eileen is bringing lunch today."

"Sweet." Sam peeled off his gloves and shoved them in his back pocket.

Finn pushed to his feet, noticing a couple spots in the fence that would need to be fixed in the days to come. "She has been doting on Ethan and the baby."

"Speaking of which." Sean Farraday stood up beside his son and ranch hand, all three eyeing the large truck making its way across the pasture. The men smiled like fools when the door opened and out popped Aunt Eileen.

"Y'all made good time this morning." She slammed the door shut with her foot.

"No water to cross. Calves kept up pretty good." Sam moved to reach for the aluminum tray. "Allow me."

As they'd done for ages and eons, the trays of warm food were spread out on the tail of the truck and one by one, Sean first, plates were filled and folks moved to sit and enjoy.

"Boy, I missed these hot lunches," Sam said.

Frowning, Eileen looked up from her plate. "It's not like you don't have a freezer stocked with my casseroles."

"Gotta admit, it's nice to have a warm meal midday to fill the belly." Finn kissed his aunt on the cheek and turned to where the others sat.

"Hmm," Aunt Eileen groused, plate in hand, leaning against the truck, "not my fault you two are still single."

"Now don't get your britches in a knot," Sean said. "Sam and Finn didn't mean anything more than we just appreciate a hearty lunch is all. Thank you."

"Yes, ma'am, Miss Eileen," Sam repeated. "No matter who I marry, she'll have a hard time competing with your cooking."

Just a hint of pink singed his aunt's cheeks and Finn thought they really didn't pay her compliments nearly often enough. "Thanks, Aunt Eileen. This is delicious."

One of the dogs began barking and Sean turned, recognizing King's yap. King was one of the best cattle dogs Finn had ever seen. The animal did the work of two men some days. Without the dogs, they'd never be able to run all the cattle with just the three of them.

The louder lowing coming from the cows along with shifting by the animals near King had Finn putting his plate on the tail of the truck and walking around to grab the rifle from the rack.

"You thinking the cows disturbed a rattler?" Aunt Eileen scanned the ground around the truck. "All these years and those things still give me the heebie jeebies."

"You're not the only one." Sam smiled at her. "Back in Wyoming, we could kill a snake with a shovel, but down here, the snakes are bigger than the shovels."

The closer Finn got to where all the ruckus was, the less of the snake jokes being told by the truck he could hear. Sam was a nice guy, he'd come to Texas a few years ago during the rodeo circuit complaining about Wyoming being cold enough to freeze a cow to the ground where it stood. After a couple of days talking and drinking, the Farradays had a new ranch hand. First time anyone not a blood relative lived or worked on the ranch, and Sam hadn't yet done anything to make Finn or his dad regret the decision.

"Yep," Finn mumbled to himself. Not quite upon the bedlam, like a pair of Latin maracas at an all-night party, the snake's rattle could be heard loud and clear. Good at their jobs, giving the rattler a wide berth, King and Bo had the few cows too indifferent to do more than give the snake a dirty look moving away from striking distance. Truth was, around this part of the country more dogs than cows got bit by snakes, and the last thing Finn wanted was for that to happen to either of the dogs.

"That'll do, Bo. That'll do, King." Like the well-trained cattle dogs they were, the two quit and hurried to Finn's side. At least real life wasn't like an old cowboy movie. He'd be able to shoot the hissing thing from where he stood and the worst that would happen is a dirty-cow-look would be flashed in his direction. The stampede of cattle because of a gunshot in the distance was all Hollywood hooey.

Not wasting time, he brought up the rifle, took aim at the angry reptile, and fired. Still squirming and wiggling, like a fish out of water, the snake hit the ground hard.

His eyes on the intruder, Finn called over his shoulder, "Hey Sam, bring me that shovel."

Shovel in hand, Sam ran up to him. "Nice shot!"

"Let's get his head chopped off and buried before one of the dogs tries to play with him and gets bit."

With a nod Sam took off a few feet to where the rattler had finally stopped moving.

Turning toward where his dad and aunt watched the excitement, Finn did a double take. Off in the distance a gray shadow streaked across the pasture. A suspiciously four-legged furry shadow.

"Oh, man. Fourteen buttons on the tail." Sam gave a low whistle. "This guy must have really made some noise. Just thinking about it makes my hair stand on end."

Finn nodded. He felt the same way, except the shiver going up his back didn't have a blessed thing to do with the rattler.

CHAPTER TWO

What was Gray doing out here? Finn strode back to where his family was finishing up lunch, replaced the rifle on the truck rack and pulled his gloves from his back pocket. "I think I'm going to head back to the house, get the four-wheeler and check out some of this fence line. We may have to deal with it before we start replacing the next pasture section."

His dad nodded. "We can handle things here."

The hard part of the morning work had been done so Finn didn't feel near as guilty as he should, wandering off in search of a strange dog. Swinging his leg over the horse and settling into the saddle, he nudged his mare's sides and turned toward the last place he'd seen the dog. Following the fence line, he'd made it all the way back to the ranch without even a single glimpse of the bewildering mutt.

"You're back early." Ethan stood on the porch, baby Brittany strapped to his front like a kangaroo Joey.

Finn never understood why all baby kangaroos were given a boy's name. Seemed like the females should've been Jane. "Noticed some fence line needing repair in today's pasture. Before we start the big project replacing the next scheduled section of fence, thought I'd better take the four-wheeler and see if any more needs securing where the cows are now."

Ethan blew out a sigh. "Sorry I can't be of any use to you yet."

"No worries." Finn stepped onto the porch and ran his knuckle against Bree's cheek. "You're liking hanging out with Daddy, aren't you?" Finn wasn't sure who had the brighter smile, Brittany or his brother. "Should you be standing on that leg?"

"Just coming in from my doctor-recommended twenty-minute

walk."

Knowing his brother's tendency to push too far too fast, Finn was willing to make a serious wager that Ethan had been walking that ankle a lot more than just twenty minutes. Finn grabbed hold of his niece's hand and wiggled it about. "Would you tell me if your Daddy was fibbing?"

Brittany's eyes grew wide before folding into the perfect frown. There was no stopping the burst of laughter that ruptured from deep in Finn's gut. Not even walking and already she had her dad's back. Yep, Farraday loyalty ran deep in this kid's blood too.

Looking down at his daughter, Ethan patted the infant gently. "Atta girl."

"Who'd of thunk." Finn stepped back and grabbed Brandy's rein.

"Why don't you let us put her away?" Ethan reached out. "Then you can get going on that fence line before dark."

"I don't—"

"Go." Ethan grabbed the reins. "We'll be fine. It's about time she got friendlier with the horses."

"How friendly?" Up until this very second, Finn had never considered if the daring streak that made his brother such a fantastic military pilot would allow Ethan to do something really stupid with Brittany.

"Not that friendly." Ethan rolled his eyes. "Go on. I promise I won't make her check Brandy's hooves without supervision."

"Don't say things like that." Now visions of his niece someday crawling under foot, or hoof, around Brandy would haunt Finn the rest of the afternoon.

On the four-wheeler, Finn cut across the open space beyond the house, taking a shortcut to the pasture where the first of the cattle had been moved days ago. Only halfway to his destination, another gray flash appeared. This time instead of bolting away, the furry enigma was running straight for him. Finn slowed the engine and came to a near halt about the same time the dog came running along side him. This close up, Gray looked more wolf than canine.

If Finn didn't know better, he'd swear the animal was trying to herd the vehicle in a different direction. "What are you up to, Gray?"

The dog's ears perked, his hind quarters flopped to the ground and something fell out of his mouth.

"What ya got there?"

Convinced the dog was going to bolt the moment Finn got within spitting distance, he was completely taken aback to see the animal remain perfectly still. When Finn stood directly in front of him, Gray barked, bent down and nudged something forward with his muzzle, then lifted his head and barked again.

Bending over to retrieve the dropped item, Finn nearly toppled over when Gray nudged Finn forward, barked repeatedly and circled in place.

"Okay, fellow. Relax."

The animal barked and circled round again.

"What the heck?" In his hand, Finn stared at a loafer. And not one that had been left out in the weather for years or decades, but a shiny leather shoe, brown, woman's size seven and a half. If he wasn't mistaken, the maker was not cheap. "Where'd you find this, boy?"

That was all Gray needed. The last word was hardly out of Finn's mouth when Gray tore off barking. The animal had galloped several yards ahead and doubled back a few feet to bark and, if Finn wasn't mistaken, wave him forward too.

"All right. I get it. You want me to follow." Finn shook his head. If he found a kid named Timmy at the bottom of a well, he'd eat the damn shoe.

Not willing to walk heaven only knew how far, Finn climbed back onto the four-wheeler and kept a steady pace behind the dog. At first Gray paused to look back at Finn, but by the time he could see the main road to the ranch in the distance, Gray had kept his eyes forward. Finn would have one hell of a time explaining the wild goose chase to his family if the only thing he finally found at the end of this parade was an empty road with no Timmy, no well, and no dog.

Except, parked by the fence, a compact gray sedan meant the dog really was after something. Finn didn't have to be a detective to know the shoe most likely belonged to at least one person associated with that car. And if the person was willing to give up a shoe to a stray dog, things could be pretty ugly. "Damn." No longer worried about keeping his distance, Finn pointed the vehicle toward the sedan and picked up speed, fearful later might be too late.

• • • •

From where she sat, Joanna could still hear the obnoxious rattle that had sent her scurrying to safety.

"Are you never going to move?" she called anxiously to the coiled creature. In her hurried efforts to get out of striking distance from the huge snake, she'd lost a shoe and almost had a heart attack when a lurking hound swooped in to pick it up and then took off across the road and downfield with it. Not that she cared about losing the shoe, even if it was her favorite pair of Anne Klein Flex loafers, but the animal had gotten so close to the venomous vermin that she'd expected the coiled snake to strike out and latch onto the poor thing and not let go.

Even if the damn snake slithered away, she still might not be in the clear. Because she'd only expected a short jaunt to this pasture and back in order to snap a couple of photos, she'd left the car door ajar. Which meant if by some miracle the battery still had enough juice to turn over by the time Mr. Rattler went home, she'd be terrified that Mrs. Rattler or a one of their relatives might have taken up residence inside the car. Not that she had anything against live and let live, she'd just rather do her living with something of a two legged and warm blooded variety.

The bark of a dog caught her attention. From the closeness of the sound, he'd been approaching for a bit, but she'd been too engrossed in worst-case death scenarios to hear him. Of course, this whole mess served her right for making fun of her sister. Linda had been right. People raised in suburbia aren't meant to go roaming around wild places like the barren west unsupervised. Or at least, unarmed. Unlike a few hours ago, she now feared she just might very well get bit by a snake and wouldn't be at all surprised to find a bobcat lurking in the distance or a renegade Indian raid come riding down on her last stand.

Okay, maybe she'd been in the Texas sun too long. There had to be a way out of this. If only she hadn't dropped her phone when she lurched back after spotting the snake. Then she could have simply called for help. Looking from left to right, she wasn't all too sure though where that help would have come from. Right about now would be the time in a good romantic western novel for the hero to ride up on his gallant steed. She glanced at the still coiled and rattling snake. Or maybe animal control would be better. Or better yet, a vet with anti-venom.

The dog gave off another woof and Joanna spotted a four-wheeler flying across the field in her direction. "Yay. The cavalry." Hopefully this rescuer was of the knights of the realm sort and came with his anti snake suit of armor. And a big-ass axe. "Over here," she called across the road.

The tall hero looked up from examining her car and tipped his hat back enough for her to spot the familiar chiseled features. Finn.

Shit. Not exactly the way she'd pictured running into him again after all these years. Once again, Finnegan Farraday to her rescue.

Spotting her, he blinked, shook his head and crossing the street, turned, looking from side to side, scanning the area. There was no missing the second he'd gotten close enough to recognize her through the leaves. His eyes circled round as full moons and his jaw dropped open.

"Close your mouth, you'll catch flies," she shouted at him.

"Joanna?"

"Hi there," she spoke casually, as though she'd been sipping mint juleps at an outdoor café, flashed her brightest smile and offered her version of a royal wave. “Long time no see, hubby.”

Tipping up the brim of his hat he looked her dead in the eye. “What the hell are you doing in that tree?”

CHAPTER THREE

Well if this didn't beat everything. Finn's hand on the top railing, he was about to duck and slip through to the other side of the fence when Joanna yelled, "Don't move. Don't come any closer." And then he heard it. The sound that had no doubt sent her up a tree.

Standing upright again, he looked to the sound. The rattler was coiled a good ten feet from the tree—a tree with a furry gray dog sitting at its base like the Sphinx of Giza.

"Hang on," he called up, then spun about and trotted back to the four-wheeler, grabbed the rifle and hurried back. He'd used this sucker more today than he had in months. Once again setting his sites on the rattler, he aimed and fired. The rattling stopped, but the snake continued to wiggle around as his cousin had done earlier this afternoon in the summer pasture. "Okay." Finn lowered the gun and looked up to her. "You can come down now."

"Yeah." She looked over to the snake then down at the dog.

"He won't hurt you."

The dog lifted his head, panting and tail wagging, and she smiled down at him. "Good boy. You brought help."

Finn wondered if she'd feel the same way once his aunt found out about the role Gray played in the little rescue. If she found out. "Come on down," he called.

"About that." She lifted her gaze to meet his and flashed another toothy smile.

He was surprised she didn't try using that grin to charm the snake. Heaven knows back in school she could charm her way into anywhere or out of anything with the bat of an eye and that sweet smile.

"Apparently running for your life makes it way easier to get up a tree than down."

It took him a few seconds to take in the lone oak and determine the way down. "Okay, you're going to have to scoot back a bit, turn around, then swing your right leg over and you should be able to reach the that limb underneath. From there it's just a short drop to the ground."

Her brows shot up and she looked down at the lower limb. "Couldn't you just go get a ladder?"

City girls. "Didn't you ever climb a tree as a kid?"

"Yes, and I always got down by jumping into Daddy's arms."

"Well that's not happening now." Finn leaned the rifle along the fence post and moved up beside the dog. His tail began swishing in earnest and Finn squatted down to scratch his ears. "You've certainly done your good deed for the day." The strangest thing. The dog seemed to nod before extending his paw. And from what Finn could tell, he didn't seem matted and tangled the way any animal out on his own this long would be. "Who do you belong to, fella?"

The dog barked and backed up.

"Excuse me," Joanna called from the tree. "I really would like to get down before the tree bark pattern is permanently etched on my derriere."

Patting the top of the dog's head, Finn shoved upright and parked himself directly below where Joanna was perched. "You're going to have to help a little. Go ahead and swing that leg over."

With a harrumph and muttering something that sounded like "stupid snake," she did as she was told, her legs dangling to one side of the large limb. "Are you sure there's a branch down there?"

He had to chuckle. "Why would I make something like that up? You saw it. Just swing your legs a bit." It took a couple of awkward movements but she got one foot then the other solidly on the lower branch—and stopped. "You're going to have to let go of that first limb. Crouch a bit to balance," he said.

"Crouch?" She turned to look over her shoulder at him. "There is no way I am letting go of this—"

That was all he heard. The next thing he knew a well-rounded 'derriere' as she'd called it, was careening toward him. Wrapping his arms around her as best he could, he bent at the knees and stumbled back until he was flat on his back with all one hundred pounds or so of Joanna Gaines sprawled across him.

Blowing a lock of hair away from her forehead, she looked down at Finn. "Not quite the way Daddy used to do it."

• • • •

"You okay?" Finn shifted and pulled a flat rock from underneath him and tossed it aside.

"Yes, I think so." She'd leaned upright so she was sort of sitting on his thighs. Again, not the way she'd expected to run into Finn Farraday.

The wolf-like dog came hurrying over, sniffed at Finn a second and then licked his face.

"Oh isn't that cute." And to think she'd been afraid when she'd first seen the animal rushing toward her. "I like your dog."

"He's not mine." Finn scratched at the animal's neck and then patted him and firmly said "away." As if used to following instructions, the dog scurried backward and Finn looked up at her. "Think you can stand?"

"Oh. Yes. Sorry." Pushing up onto her feet, she climbed off him. "I don't suppose the dog that isn't yours left my shoe somewhere near by?"

"In my four-wheeler." Finn stood and leaned over, his hands holding his knees, he took in a few deep breaths.

"Maybe I should be the one asking if you're all right?" She reached out and splayed her hand across his back. "I guess I'm a little heavier than I was at six."

"A little?" Still bending over he lifted his face to look at her, his eyes twinkling. "So what brings you to this part of the world?"

"Work."

He straightened. "What kind of work?"

"I'm doing an article on West Texas ghost towns."

"Hasn't that been done already?"

"I'll do it better." Speaking of work, she hoped her camera survived the drop when she took off for the tree. "I need to find my phone and my camera."

As if on cue, her phone beeped low battery and she trotted one-shoed in the direction of the sound, spotted it easily in the golden grass, and snatched it up. A couple of feet further lay her camera.

"Does it work?"

Joanna lifted the camera and snapped a photograph of Finn standing with the sunlight behind him. His blue shirt rolled up at the arms, a buckle big as the state of Texas holding up not quite tight jeans and the required rancher boots completed the picture perfect cowboy snapshot. "Yep. Still works."

"So were you planning on passing through and not giving me a call?"

"Nope." She stuck her phone in her pocket and slung her camera over her shoulder. "Was on my way to your ranch. At least I think I am." She snorted a chuckle. "Don't have much faith in GPS out here and of course without a house number."

Shaking his head, Finn laughed outright. "No one needs numbers or GPS out here."

"I'll remember that." She moved closer to where he stood. "So am I going to get a chance to see this ranch of yours and get a taste of West Texas hospitality?"

"You bet." He leaned over and picked up his hat. "I'm pretty sure I heard Aunt Eileen say she was baking blueberry pies today."

"Oh, my. I remember the time she left a care package after a Parents Weekend. Best damn pies ever."

Finn grinned and nodded. "Absolutely. So, you want to follow me back?"

"Sounds like a plan. If the car starts."

He raised a brow at her.

"I may have left the door open."

"Okay." He shrugged and smiled. The guy knew her too well. "If it doesn't start right away you can ride with me and we'll come back later for it."

She was about to say she'd have to at least bring her laptop because she didn't want someone stealing it when she realized she hadn't seen a car on the road for hours, and smiled instead. "Don't have to worry about thieves, do I?"

"Nope." Finn looked around, frowned then looked around again. "He did it again."

"Who, did what?" She followed his gaze.

"The dog."

She didn't see the friendly animal either. "Where is he?"

"That's what he does." Finn blew out a sigh. "You wait here and I'll go get your other shoe."

"Nah," she waved him off. "I made it up a tree with one shoe, I can make across the road."

Finn's head tipped, his smile broadened. "It's nice to see you. You're looking good, JoJo."

"You're not looking so bad yourself." She couldn't help grinning back. "Not bad at all, hubby."

CHAPTER FOUR

"Just park anywhere," Finn called out and climbed off the four-wheeler in front of the house, waving Joanna over. He wasn't sure what was the biggest surprise of the day, the dog showing up, finding a woman in a tree, or discovering the woman was Joanna.

How many years had it been? Five? Six? He'd lost track of time since graduating, but it didn't matter, Joanna looked exactly the same. Sassy, spirited, with a penchant for getting herself into trouble. And somehow after all these years she'd still pulled him smack dab into the middle of her most recent shenanigans.

He trotted around the hood in time to open her door.

"Always the gentleman." She turned and looked at the house. "Wow."

Finn slammed the car door behind her.

Staring slack jaw, Joanna didn't move. "Exactly the way you'd described it."

"It is what it is."

"No." She smiled wide. "*This* is more than a hundred years of Farradays."

He had to nod. She was right. For a city girl she got what this place meant to him. The large ranch house was more than a home, more than brick and mortar. It was in many ways the lifeline between once upon a time and now. Both things he was very proud of. "Come on inside. And remember, do not say a word about the dog to my aunt."

"I still don't understand why not, but—"

"Think of this as payback for all the times I had to play along with you."

"You didn't *have* to." She scrunched her face at him. "Deep down you're just a big ham."

Finn stepped onto the front porch first. "And don't forget talented. We were never called out on it."

"Well," Joanna came to a stop beside him as he pushed the front door open, "there was that one time that we sort of almost started a teeny," she held up her hand and pinched her fingers, "little brawl."

Door open, Finn ushered her inside. Many nights of collegiate partying long forgotten flooded back to mind, but nothing about a brawl. "You may have to refresh my memory, I seem to have forgotten."

"Forgotten what?" Aunt Eileen looked up from the living room and springing to her feet, hurried to meet them. "Oh, hello." His aunt squinted slightly at her guest before smiling with recognition.

"You remember Joanna?" Finn figured he'd better help out with the name just in case. "Joanna, this is my Aunt Eileen."

"Yes, I remember well," Joanna said.

"It's been too long, dear." She stepped sideways and motioned for Joanna to move forward. "What brings you to these parts?"

"I'm working on a travel article about the surrounding ghost towns."

"You were serious?" He'd known Joanna for three of his four years in college. She'd studied Psychology with a minor in Biology. Smart as she was social. With scientific credentials like that, how did she wind up writing? And about ghost towns? In West Texas.

"Well, we're not going to gab about it standing here. Make yourselves comfortable and I'll get a little refreshment."

"No need to put yourself out," Joanne said.

"She won't rest until you ask for something. You might as well give in now." Finn loved his aunt very much, but the woman was bound and determined to make everyone happy. Whether that meant with a cool beverage, or a warm pie, or a ghostly matchmaking dog didn't matter. Whatever the dilemma, his aunt was willing to provide the solution.

"Tea? Lemonade?" Aunt Eileen offered.

"Lemonade?" Joanna's eyes had widened with interest.

Aunt Eileen smiled. "Fresh squeezed."

"Oh my." Joanna rubbed her hands at her sides. "I don't know that I've ever had lemonade that wasn't powdered or frozen first."

"Then lemonade coming up." Aunt Eileen took a step toward the kitchen. " Finn, you too?"

Finn looked around. "Where's Ethan and the baby?"

"Taking a nap."

"Ethan?" Since when did his Marine brother take naps?

Aunt Eileen shrugged. "The baby went down and I made him go to his room as well and put his foot up."

Now that made sense. "Good. I know he was on that leg too long today."

"I, for one, will be happy when Allison returns from that East Coast conference. It's getting so that she's the only one who can keep him in line."

Finn couldn't help but chuckle. His aunt had a point. They'd all noticed how in a few short weeks Ethan had gone from macho man to domestic don. "Don't worry. A few more years and Brittany will be riding roughshod over him too."

Shaking her head, his aunt laughed. "I don't doubt you're right one little bit." Then she turned to the kitchen.

"I forgot how much I liked your aunt."

"Everyone loves Aunt Eileen." Finn couldn't help but smile.

Joanna curled her feet under her and took in the high ceilings in the large family room. "There's so much space."

"You know what they say, everything is big in Texas. Well, even more so here in West Texas. Bigger hats, bigger belts—"

"Bigger egos?" she teased.

"Nah," he smiled. "Our good looks and cunning wit speak for themselves."

"Oh, yeah," she laughed. "Still humble."

Finn joined her laughing. He'd forgotten how easily she made him relax and just enjoy the moment. "So how long you planning on being in the area?"

"Not sure. What I'd really like is to write something that's got a little personal story to it besides the facts. Dig into some of the folklore and bring them to life along with the pictures."

"Which explains the camera?"

"It's not a major article so all I need is one or two good shots. If it were something more prestigious like the cover, then I'd get a pro."

Aunt Eileen walked into the room and set a tray with three lemonades on the coffee table.

"And when is all this set to happen?" Finn asked, reaching for his drink. Funny, she'd just sat down in his living room and already he was missing his old friend about to take off on another adventure.

"Oh, thank you." Joanna took a sip and sighed. "Totally delish."

"Glad you like it." Aunt Eileen took a seat and her own drink.

Joanna set her glass on the table. "Like I said, I'm not really sure. I don't want the stories I can read at the library. I want a story that hasn't been in print before. Something that only descendants of former residents of the old towns would know."

"Not a tall order at all." Finn shifted forward in his seat. "And where do you expect to find these descendants?"

"Not—"

"Sure," he finished for with a chuckle.

"Oh, that'll be easy," Aunt Eileen said quickly.

"How is that?" Finn turned to his aunt. "Are you going to tell me the Callahans came from one of the abandoned towns?"

"Of course not," she waved him off. "Where does anyone go to find out all the gossip that ever was for the county?"

At the same moment, Finn and his aunt echoed, "Sisters."

• • • •

Joanna had no idea who the sisters were but she was getting goose flesh at the first possible break for her idea.

"Those two know everything about everyone. If there's a story to be told, they'll know it. And if they don't, they'll know who will."

"So who knows their real names?" Finn asked.

"Their real names?" That didn't make sense to Joanna.

Finn nodded. "My entire life they've been Sister and Sissy. They've run the equivalent of the general store here for just as long."

"And their parents ran it before them," Aunt Eileen tilted her head at him. "If you're so curious, ask them."

"Not that curious." He sat back.

Joanna didn't know what the big deal was, but she'd forgotten how cute Finn looked when he was out of his comfort zone. He was the quiet one of the group. Approaching people, even people she didn't know, and drumming up conversation was her thing, not his. "If you don't think they'd mind talking to me, I'd love to sit down and interview them."

"Mind?" Aunt Eileen shrugged. "Nothing those two like better than a captive audience. And I bet Ned might know a story or two. He's probably old enough to have lived in a ghost town himself!"

"Could be," Finn agreed easily.

"What could be?" Joanna recognized the tall man who'd just walked into the room in what had to be the West Texas cowboy uniform as Finn's dad. With twinkling blue eyes and sharp features, he looked like Finn might in another thirty years or so.

"That Ned is older than dirt," Aunt Eileen stood and smiled at the man. "I'll get you a lemonade. In the meantime, you remember Finn's friend Joanna from A&M."

"Nice to see you." Mr. Farraday smiled and Joanna knew from whom Finn had gotten his disarming grin. Finn could have charmed the panties off every co-ed on campus if he'd been so inclined, but the guy bled honor and respect before Aggie maroon.

"You too." She never knew if she was supposed to stand up or offer her hand or what. She went to stand up and Finn's dad waved her off.

"Please don't get up. And if anyone really wants to know, yes Ned is older than dirt."

"See. I'm sure we can find plenty of stories for you, dear." Aunt Eileen practically wiggled in her seat with excitement. "So, where will you be staying?"

Her original plans for this trip to drive along and stop wherever the mood struck her had died last night. At the only motel for miles, she'd slept fully clothed on—not in—the bed and while she hadn't felt the need to shove a chair under the doorknob for security, she hadn't gotten much sleep. "I need to look into my nearest options. I remember a new bed and breakfast in a town not far from here, but it doesn't have much history yet."

"That's my sister-in-law Meg's place."

"Oh, well. In that case—"

"In that case you'll stay here with us." Aunt Eileen stood from her seat and dipped her chin in a single motion that said there'd be no argument.

Joanna turned to Finn and palms up he smiled and shook his head slightly. "Guess you have a place to stay."

CHAPTER FIVE

"This pie is so much better than I remembered." Joanna took another bite.

Finn shook his head and smiled. Even though she'd had two slices at dinner, now, way past his bedtime, with the entire family gone to bed, the two of them sat in the kitchen having a late night snack. He still expected to awaken any minute in bed and discover this entire crazy day had been nothing more than one extremely far-fetched dream. "You should know, that's your third piece."

"Fourth if you count the one your aunt gave me before dinner." She waved a forkful of blueberry at him. "Besides, currants are filled with anti-oxidants, they're good for me."

"Right. So is all that sugar." Finn picked a blueberry from her plate. "So tell me, how did a nice girl like you turn a psych degree into a writing career?"

Joanna toyed with the berries on her plate. "I knew from the start of school that I'd need at least five years postgrad to do anything with my degree. That was okay because I always figured if I lost steam with my bio credits I could fall back on teaching science."

"Plan B. Yes, I remember."

"Well, turns out that therapists aren't allowed to tell their patients to shit or get off the pot, and I'm not terribly fond of thirty tenth-grade biology students several hours a day, five days a week, for nine months a year."

Neither one of those results surprised Finn. "But writing? As I remember you did nothing but bitch and moan over every paragraph that ever had to be written for English Lit."

"Turns out writing is way more appealing if it includes a

paycheck." She stabbed at another morsel of pie. "And as fate would have it, it also turns out I'm good."

That he didn't doubt. "So you started writing for travel magazines?"

Joanna snorted. "Not hardly. I read a book that ticked me off so I sat down and wrote a short story with an end more to my liking. Then I progressed to some freelance articles for the local paper which led into a pretty steady gig for *Texas Travel* magazine, and in my spare time, I made an attempt at the great American novel."

"How'd that work out for you?"

"I'll know if I ever get past page one."

"Page one?"

"I've actually written more." Joanna shrugged, "All boring. So in the meantime, I write for whoever will pay me, including the occasional piece for the lifestyle section of my local paper. If you ever make it to the Dallas area and pick up a newspaper, you're bound to find something with my name on it."

"Next time I'll pay more attention."

"My byline is J. M. Gaines"

"J.M.?" Finn didn't understand. "You don't use your full name? Is it a masculine puff sort of thing?"

"More like self-preservation. Do you watch reality TV?"

"I barely watch TV, not going to watch a bunch of people running around the world, fighting through the jungles, or sharing a small house."

Joanna set the fork down and shook her head at him. "Not those shows. There's a popular home remodeling show with a married couple here in Texas. The star's name is Joanna Gaines. You have no idea how many people become incredibly irate when they meet me in person and discover I'm not 'the' Joanna Gaines. Restaurants are the worst. I'm always afraid someone's going spit on my food for revenge."

"So you go by your initials to avoid any conflict."

"Exactly!" She swallowed the last mouthful. "If your aunt

makes pie like this every day I am going to be in serious trouble."

"You can work it off like the rest of us, breakfast is at five—"

"Five? No wonder farm people—"

"We're ranchers."

"I stand corrected." She smiled. "You ranchers go to bed with the chickens."

He almost spit out his aunt's common retort—we don't have chickens—but instead he went with, "Fence riding begins at first light."

"On the four-wheeler?"

"Sometimes, but tomorrow we'll be on horseback."

Her face lit up. "Really?"

Finn had to laugh. "Of course really."

"No, I understand you're really going to be on horseback, I mean can I ride the fence?"

He hadn't meant his comment to be an invitation, and even if he had, he wouldn't have expected her to take him up on it. "You know how to ride a horse?"

"Does the merry-go-round at Fair Park count?" she grinned coyly.

"Not exactly. Besides, I thought you were going to go to town and talk to the sisters?"

"I think it would be fun to see what you do in person." She stood and carried the empty plate to the sink.

Finn did the same and reached for the dish soap. "I'll take care of those."

"Now I understand why you were the only neat guy in the apartment." Joanna retreated to the table and returned with two empty glasses.

"You mean I was the only neat *person* in the apartment. As I remember it, you and I were the only ones who even knew how to turn on a vacuum cleaner."

"Not true. Terri could turn it on no problem, she just didn't know quite what to do with it after that. So I can come with you in the morning?"

"Tomorrow we'll be fixing broken chunks of fence wire in one of the summer pastures. It's boring and slow moving riding from post to post. You'll have a much more interesting time in town." Finn closed the door to the dishwasher and turned the machine on.

"I can hit town in the afternoon."

Heaven knows what came over Finn, but instead of insisting that heading out to the pasture with him and his dad would not be a good idea, he'd nodded and heard himself say, "Five o'clock comes around awfully fast. We'd better call it a night."

• • • •

Oh boy, Finn wasn't kidding. Five in the morning came around too fast. And it wasn't that she had to be out of bed at five in the morning. Joanna had to be out of bed, dressed and seated at the table by five am.

"Don't you look bright-eyed and bushy-tailed." Aunt Eileen smiled over her shoulder from her position in front of the stove.

Already the table was covered by plates stacked with pancakes, toast, scrambled eggs, bacon, and holding a skillet, Aunt Eileen turned and piled hash brown potatoes onto the lone empty dish on the table. Joanna could feel her arteries clogging. Even more surprising was the amount of food loaded onto Finn and his dad's plate.

It had taken Joanna a few long minutes to notice the extra person at the table. At first she thought it was the brother with the baby and then she realized, while clearly the guy carried the same Farraday DNA, this was a new person to her.

"Jo, this is my brother Connor. He's going to be helping out today."

"Nice to meet you." The brother, Connor, flashed a bright smile, also clearly part of the Farraday DNA, and then returned to the steak and eggs on his plate.

"Would you like some coffee, dear?" Aunt Eileen asked.

“Be warned,” Finn looked up from his own cup, “it will put hair on your chest.”

Joanna spotted the orange bottle on the counter. She liked coffee with a lot of sugar and even more cream, but she was pretty sure she wasn’t up to cowboy coffee. “Juice will be fine, thank you.”

Filled juice glass in hand, Joanna took a seat, scooped up a spoonful of eggs and a slice of toast.

“Oh, if you’re going to work with us, you’ll have to eat more than that.” Finn took a bite and Joanna noticed biscuits and gravy were also part of the morning menu.

“I don’t usually eat much in the morning.”

“You also don’t usually repair a fence line. “ Finn took a sip of coffee and she could see Mr. Farraday and Connor paying way too much attention to cutting the food on their plates. “Trust me when I tell you that you’re gonna want something that will stick to your ribs until lunchtime.”

“Finn’s right.” Aunt Eileen set down a plate of warm ham in front of her. “Protein is good, but carbs are energy.” A second later another plate of warm biscuits appeared in front of her. “Try the biscuits. Made from scratch and the strawberry jam too.”

“You’ll want to try the biscuit with just butter first.” Finn passed her a butter dish. Only this butter wasn’t a nice cubed shape, it was a thick slab on a round dish. “One of the neighbors down the road a piece sells fresh butter. You should try it.”

Not wanting to appear difficult, she did as she was told. All it took was one bite for her to nearly moan with delight. “Oh, wow.”

The head of the family chuckled to himself, and Connor’s smile spread from ear to ear. “My wife is from Chicago. We made a deal long before our wedding day. She gets to sleep until after the sun comes up and I’ll keep having breakfast at the ranch. She insists, unlike ranchers, lawyers don’t need the extra calories.”

“You live close?”

Connor nodded. “Next place over. About a mile door to door.”

"I guess that's close in this part of the state."

All three heads nodded. Then, taking his last bite, Finn stood and picking up his plate and coffee cup, walked over to the sink. His aunt was already cleaning up the mess and Finn gave her a peck on the cheek. "Delicious as always. You're the best, Aunt Eileen." Setting the dirty dishes down, he turned to the folks at the table.

Joanna was doing her utmost to shovel down the protein to go with the biscuits, but she didn't really think she could eat another bite. Picking up her plate, she stood as well. "I'm ready whenever you are."

Finn took inventory of Joanna from neck to toe. "The clothes are fine, but the loafers are going to have to go. Did you bring boots?"

Joanna looked down to her feet. She lived in Dallas most of the time, not Fort Worth. "No."

"What size are you, honey?" Aunt Eileen moved over and put a hand on her shoulder.

"Seven and a half."

"That'll be Grace. I wear a seven. She wears an eight. Double socks will work." Aunt Eileen turned to Finn.

"Already on my way," he said.

Five minutes later she looked and felt like a real cowgirl. Including the hat Aunt Eileen had given her for the sun.

"You're all set." Aunt Eileen grinned at her as if she were a child ready for her first day of school.

She followed Finn and his brother out the door and to the barn. Inside he walked straight to a tan horse with a white mane.

"This is Princess," Finn said. "She's pretty easygoing. You should do fine on her."

"How do you do?" Joanna stepped slightly to the side, near Finn, before running her hand down Princess' head. "You're a pretty girl. Anyone ever tell you that?" The horse snorted and dipped her head and Joanna laughed. "Oh, yeah. We're going to get along just fine."

Finn slipped the halter over Princess' head and led her out into the aisle between the stalls.

Once he'd secured Princess in the crossties, Finn handed Joanna a brush. "Brush all the dirt off, and definitely any burrs you find. I'll get her saddled up for you soon as I get Brandy fixed up."

"No need. I can do it."

Finn raised a brow. "No. I'll do it." He walked away and returned with a couple of saddle pads with blankets, set them on a nearby bale of hay and turned around again.

Joanna was pretty sure that having her here today was going to slow him down some anyhow and she didn't want to delay the others any more than she had to. Placing the pad on Princess' back first, she placed one of the blankets over it, carefully lining it up.

Saddle in his arms, Finn walked up to her. "What are you doing?"

"Getting Princess ready."

Looking at the horse, over to where he'd set the pad down and back, Finn blew out a sigh. "I know you want to help. But you've got to be careful around horses. Even the good ones. We don't want to start the day with a horse getting spooked, and I most certainly don't want you getting hurt. If we're going to be working today, I need you to promise you'll do as I say."

Joanna had to think about that one a minute longer than Finn probably liked. She'd never been one to do as she was told, and Finn had never been one to try and boss her around, so this was new territory for them. But this was his ranch and his horses.

"Promise," she said.

Finn lifted a brow at her. "Promise what?"

"To do exactly as I'm told." She resisted the urge to cross her fingers behind her back. There was, after all, a first time for everything.

CHAPTER SIX

Finn set the saddle on the ground, reached out and lifting the corner of the blanket, checked underneath. Not bad, but even a city slicker could have easily figured out what the pad and blanket were for. Though they may not have gotten them in the right order. But Princess' hide gleamed beneath. She'd done a good job brushing.

"Excuse me." Joanna stood slightly behind him, the saddle in her hands, far side stirrup resting over the seat.

"Hey." He moved forward. "That's heavy."

"Yes. Which is why I'd like you to move over so I can set this on her."

Finn reached for the saddle and had to give a slightly harder than expected tug for Joanna to release her hold. "Not just for you, but for the horse." He let the saddle fall easily onto Princess' back. Then walked around to straighten the girths. "You don't want sixty pounds of saddle to come down heavy on her back," he said over his shoulder.

"No." She agreed easily. Perhaps too easily.

By the time he'd walked back around to where Joanna stood, she'd leaned under, pulled the front cinch toward her and tightened it under the horse, waiting as the mare expelled her breath. He'd caught a glimpse of her hands as she checked the buckle and then continued to wrap the cinch strap until she ran out of length. Curious now, he paused and in silence watched her snug it up and lock in the buckle. As she took a step along and reached for the back cinch, he crossed his arms and stepped up beside her.

She buckled the back strap and stuck her hand between it and the horse's belly, checking it wasn't too tight, then reached for the mare's bridle hanging on a hook. As easily as he could have done himself, she replaced the halter with the bridle. The mare accepted the bit easily and Joanna straightened the mare's forelock and checked that the cheekpiece wasn't too tight. Crossing her arms the way he had done moments before, she turned to face him.

"You've done this before." It wasn't a question.

"Yeah." She nodded casually. "You could say that."

"Then you know how to ride?" It was a stupid question. No one learned how to saddle a horse without ever learning to ride. It wasn't like the pit crew of a race car that might never learn to drive.

"It's been a while." She patted the horse's jaw. "Growing up, my parents had a timeshare in the Dominican Republic. It was only one week a year, but I loved it."

"You never mentioned that before."

"You never asked."

Why would he? Who would have thought a gal who freely admitted to being born and raised in suburban Dallas would know anything at all about horses? In all the late night conversations that might have included him talking about the ranch or the cattle, never did she give even the tiniest hint that she had a clue about any aspect of his life. "Would I be correct in guessing you don't need a leg up?"

Joanna flashed him one of her I-know-more-than-you smiles, grabbed the horn, slipped her foot into the stirrup and swinging herself up and her leg over, settled easily onto the saddle. "Nope."

Reins in hand, she tightened her knees against the horse. "I'll wait for you outside."

He'd been had. Which would explain why she'd lit up like a Christmas tree at the mention of riding today. Watching Joanna's back as the horse ambled out of the barn, her hips balancing from side to side with Princess' shifting rump, Finn wondered how many more surprises Joanna might have in store for him.

• • • •

"Hold on to that." Finn handed Joanna the extra wire.

It had taken all of fifteen minutes or so for the men to realize that not only would Joanna not be a hindrance to their day, she would very likely help their progress. Not that she had a clue about mending fences.

"This wasn't nearly as difficult as I'd thought it was going to be." An hour or two ago she wouldn't have braved making such a statement. Since Finn had said this was the last post and she'd made it through without losing a finger or passing out from lack of sustenance—she really should have had more breakfast—she figured she couldn't jinx herself now. Besides, she was actually pretty darn proud of herself.

"Don't stab me with anything, but you're a heck of a lot stronger than you look."

"Glad to know the gym membership wasn't a waste of money."

Finn laughed. "Not if you plan to spend a lot of time repairing cattle fences. And that," Finn secured the other end of the tightened wire, "should be that."

"So now what?" She pushed upright and hoped her face didn't show the pull in her muscles.

"Now we head back to the house for lunch. Working in two teams today we knocked this fence out and tomorrow we start on the new fence."

"New fence?"

"Yeah. Pasture by empty pasture, one at a time, we've been upgrading the fencing. These old wooden posts are always needing repair. As cows rotate out of a pasture we've been ripping them out and replacing them with modern concrete fencing."

"Makes sense."

Finn laughed again. "Glad you approve."

"Sorry," She sucked in a breath and reached for the pliers she'd left on the ground. "I didn't mean to—"

"I know, JoJo. You're still too much fun to tease."

"Some things never change." She'd never worked a fence line

with him before, but it wasn't much different from studying English or doing dishes. They'd always made a good team.

He grinned up at her. "No, they don't."

"How did we let so much time go by?" Joanna really missed her friend.

"In an age of Internet and cell phones anyone would think staying in touch would be easier." Finn scooped up the stray tools and shrugged. "What is it they say, life is what happens while we're busy making other plans."

"Ain't that the truth." Writing stories about tourist sites and roaming ghost towns of West Texas had not been anywhere even in the footnotes of her life plans. "Except you've always known this is what you wanted to do."

Walking back to where the horses were ground tied, Finn nodded. "Since I was old enough to ride a horse I knew that I never wanted to live anywhere else. Do anything else. "

"Do you have any idea how lucky you are?"

"Maybe." He swung his leg over the horse, settled in the saddle and looked her straight in the eyes. "But nothing is all that it seems."

Most of the ride back to the ranch house, Joanna wondered what he meant by that. Riding at a respectable pace across Texas flat lands was not conducive to chatting. By the time they approached the barns, the pace had slowed to an easy gait so there'd be no need to walk the horses if they were to be put up for the day. "What do you mean, nothing is all that it seems?"

Finn shrugged. "Nothing ominous. You're right. This has always been my dream, and I'm pretty much living it. I didn't have to work for years in the oil fields to buy this place nor did I have to spend a bunch more years in school to doctor people or animals."

"I sense a but coming."

"Not really. I do what I love but shit still happens."

"Like what?"

"I love my Aunt Eileen, but I'd like to have memories of my mother."

Joanna's heart twisted. She should have kept her fat mouth shut.

"My niece Stacey was in a car accident that kept her silent for too long." Finn slowed the pace a little more. "Thankfully Connor and the horses brought her out of it."

"Well, that's good then."

Finn nodded. "Cycle of life is hard to escape here. We bring animals into the world and occasionally we lose a few. Some to natural causes, some to rustlers."

"They still have cattle rustlers?" That surprised her.

"Absolutely. A lot of it is prevented at time of sale with strict rules and inspections, but it still happens and it's never good."

No, she didn't bet it was. "You've lost cattle to rustlers?"

"Not for a while." He shrugged. "I'm not saying we don't have a good life here, I'm just saying that no one's life is a Hollywood musical."

The barn was a short distance ahead and Joanna considered his words. She was pretty sure there was something else he wasn't telling her, but she was also pretty sure that her serious and quiet cowboy needed to be brought out of his shell. Again.

• • • •

Pulling into the barn, Finn slid off his horse and would have smacked himself upside the head if he could. Why in heaven's name did he say anything at all to Joanna? She was right. He was living his dream. The ranch wasn't completely his, all the brothers had a share in it, but Finn and his dad had the bulk of the responsibilities and Finn was perfectly happy with that. The ranch was all he'd ever wanted.

Even when his brothers started one by one falling for women just like the brothers in their mom's favorite movie, Finn loved the ranch and his life. He still had more plans for expansion and modernization and all of it took time, patience, dedication, and didn't leave much time for a love life, never mind a wife. Besides, now he had a sweet baby niece to fuss over without any of the burdens of parenting. His life was all good. He wasn't lonely at all.

Uncinching the strap under his horse, he glanced over at Joanna doing the same as if she too had been born and raised here. If life was so good, why did looking at her make him feel like life was all wrong?

CHAPTER SEVEN

The first inkling that soaking in a hot tub would have been a much better idea than coming into town struck Joanna when she'd stood from the lunch table and her thighs protested. Painfully. Finn had noticed her taking a few careful steps to loosen up and suggested instead of pushing forward that she stay home and take a long soak. Not wanting to look like a wuss, she'd blown the suggestion off with a wave and a chuckle and followed him to the truck.

Climbing out of the truck an hour later, her thighs, calves *and* backside all screamed.

"You do realize you're moving at the pace of my great granny?" Finn held out a hand to her and patiently waited for her to swing both legs off the side of the seat and then, shaking his head, grabbed hold of her waist and lifted her from the truck onto the ground. "You steady enough for me to let go?"

"Of course I am." Except the second his hands released their grip, her knees protested and she came within seconds of falling flat on her face and making a total ass of herself.

"Whoa." His hands tightened again and this time he waited for her to take a minced step before letting go again. "You're going to have to walk it off."

"Yeah. Give me a minute here and I'll be fine." She glanced up the quaint town square and then down the other side. "Which way is Sisters?"

Finn waved his thumb over his shoulder. "About four stores up."

"Okay." Every step came a little easier. If she wasn't in so much pain, she'd have laughed at the careful way Finn walked beside her, trying not to let on he was watching her every step.

"I'm not going to break."

"I'm not worried about you breaking. Or even falling. It's the landing I'm concerned with."

"Ha ha ha. I'm fine. Just got a little stiff not moving for so long." In retrospect, riding a horse all morning after years of not riding was probably not the smartest move she'd ever made.

Finn stopped in front of a cute little boutique and held the door open. "Whatever you say. But you may want to rethink that soak in the tub when we get back to the ranch."

There was no need to rethink anything. If she still felt like this after another hour-long ride back to the ranch, she might very well spend the whole night in the tub.

At the sound of the overhead bell, two women scurried forward. One tall and thin, the other not so much.

"Well if it isn't Finnegan Farraday. What a surprise this is." The tall skinny one with slightly reddish hair pulled him into a tight squeeze and then, lifting his chin with one finger and examining his profile as though studying a piece of art—or a horse for purchase—she nodded and grinned. "You're getting handsomer every day."

"Thank you, ma'am."

"I'm telling you, Sissy," the short and stout woman pinched his cheek, "there isn't an ugly gene in that Farraday DNA."

Pink flushed bright on Finn's face and Joanna bit back a smile of her own. As well as she and Finn had known each other, this was a new side for her. Of course, back in the day, not many eccentric sisters wandered about campus pinching his cheeks.

"So," the tall one stepped back and looked to Joanna, "going to introduce us to your lady friend?"

"Sorry," he removed his hat. "Joanna Gaines—"

"No relation," Joanna quickly provided when both sisters' eyes rounded like a cartoon owl.

"No," the tall one said, "I would think not. You're much prettier. I'm Sissy."

"And I'm Sister," the other sibling with hair almost as wide as it was high, chimed in.

"What can we do for you?" the two echoed.

"Actually," Joanna shifted her weight and tried not to groan at the discomfort coursing through her muscles. "I'm writing an article—"

"Writing?" Sister perked up.

Joanna nodded. "About a few of the local ghost towns and I was hoping some folks around here might know a little more about the history and the people."

"Well, mama's people came from Three Corners, but we don't really know too many stories." Sissy shrugged. "What kind of stories were you interested in?"

"Anything really. Something to spark an idea."

"I think it was our great great grandmother who was the first to come to Texas. Back then Three Corners had begun to really grow. Miss Lilibeth, our great great grandmother, came here from Boston."

"Boston?"

"That's right. The men folk had built a proper town and they were wanting to settle it. They'd heard about folks on the West Coast bringing in wagon trains of brides, so they did the same."

"Your great great grandmother was a mail order bride?"

"She was. Her sister Esther came with her. But Esther's intended passed on while she was traveling so she married another fellow and moved on. To California, I think."

Possibilities ricocheted in Joanna's mind. Everyone loved mail order bride stories.

The front door opened and the overhead bell rang again. Two men in uniform strolled in.

"Aren't we blessed today. Not one but two Farradays. Your uniforms came in this morning." She turned and pointed to a back cabinet and Sister hurried across the store.

"Thank you, Miss Sissy." Judging by the matching chiseled features, Joanna guessed this one was the other Farraday. Shifting sideways, the man from the same Farraday mold spotted Finn.

"Hey, bro. What brings you into town?"

"My friend wanted to talk to the sisters." Finn turned to her. "Joanna, this is my brother DJ and officer Reed Taylor."

"How do you do?" She extended her hand to one officer, then the other and kept her grin to herself when they each removed their hats. Apparently that gentleman thing ran deep and strong in this part of the country.

"Joanna's writing about ghost towns," Sissy provided.

"And we're going to help," the other added gleefully, handing DJ a package wrapped in brown paper like a Chinese laundry.

The brother's brows lifted with curiosity as his gaze drifted from the sister to Finn and then her. But it was the other officer running his fingers along the rim of his hat that caught her attention. He'd smiled and been polite, but he had a lost boy look that made the writer in her want to know the rest of the story.

"We've got boxes in the attic with old photos and things." The plump, more animated sister turned to her sibling. "Don't we, Sissy?"

"That's right. I haven't looked in those old trunks since we were kids." Sissy looked to Joanna. "You'd be welcome to come look through anything if you want."

"Oh, that would be really cool. Thank you. Very much."

The sister beamed at her reaction. "We're closed on Sundays. Any time after church would be fine."

Excitement gurgled inside her. This was going to happen. Her little idea was blossoming into a fantastic idea. "I'll make that happen."

Finn laughed softly. "I bet you will. I just bet you will."

• • • •

Leaving his brother and Reed at Sisters, Finn escorted Joanna across the way to Ned's garage, pleased to see her moving a little more easily. "Ned is seriously older than dirt, but if he has to, the man can fix anything that has a motor with chewing gum and rubber bands."

"Sounds like the perfect mechanic."

Finn stepped onto the curb. "He is, and if he ever dies, the whole town is screwed."

"He can't be the only mechanic in town."

"No, but he's the best." Finn pulled the door open and waited for her to go inside.

"Well how-dee-do." Ned wiped his hands on a rag. "That truck giving you trouble again?"

"No. Not here for ranch business. Ned, this is a friend of mine, Joanna Gaines."

The old man's eyes rounded with interest the same way the sisters' had and Finn realized that maybe he did need to watch a little more television.

"No relation," Joanna quickly explained. "But I'm here doing research for a story I'm working on about the West Texas ghost towns."

"Really?" Ned shoved the rag into his pocket. "Which town? There's quite a few in these parts. Some recognized, some ignored."

"Well," she inched forward, "that depends. I'm looking for some good stories."

"Oh, that won't be hard. There's lots of folks in Tuckers Bluff whose people came from one of the nearby abandoned towns."

Joanna's eyes twinkled with excitement. "Yours?"

Ned flashed a huge grin with multiple missing teeth. "You bet. All the way back to my great great grand pappy. Came here from Ireland. Don't think he meant to stop in Texas. He was heading for the California lowlands, but they'd been running behind and winter blew in early so they didn't dare cross the mountains. By the time spring had come around, most of the folks decided it was just easier to stay put."

"Which town was this?"

"Three Corners"

"Oh, the same as the sisters?"

"That's right." Ned scratched the top of his head. "Think one of the sisters' aunts was supposed to marry one of my kin, but he died 'fore she got to Texas."

"Do you know what happened to Three Corners? Or how your family wound up here in Tuckers Bluff instead?"

"Lots of things, I'm sure. My kin were farmers. Not easy out this way. As years passed, irrigation became an expensive problem. Eventually they gave up on farming and moved closer to Tuckers Bluff, but I can't speak for the rest of the town. Don't even know what year the last of the town moved away. Coulda been WWII or the hippies for all I know. Lord knows by the sixties times had really changed. Folks didn't want the quiet life. Young people wanted the bright lights of big cities."

"Did you want the big city? The bright lights?" she asked softly.

Finn was surprised to see a slight blush tinge old Ned's cheeks.

"Young men dream, but once I met my Gert, Tuckers Bluff was home for good." A far off look that might have taken Ned back to a day and time long ago settled in his gaze for a few long seconds before he shook his head and smiled at Joanna. "Gert was real good about keeping track of family. Her sister called her the family historian."

The way Joanna's eyes opened wide, Finn knew Ned had said the magic words.

"I would love to hear anything you remember about your people and Three Corners."

"It'd be my pleasure to tell a pretty girl what little this old man remembers. I've got this engine I have to rebuild for Paul Brady, but as soon it's done I'll have plenty of free time to sit and visit. You stop by in a few days and we'll get us some Dr. Peppers, sit out front and pretend it's eighteen eighty again."

"Thank you. I'd love that."

"The pleasure will be all mine, missy. I promise you that." With a nod and another toothless grin, Ned returned to the old truck up in the air.

Outside, standing on the curb, Joanna turned to Finn. “Your aunt was right. There’s a potential wealth of information here.”

Finn had to laugh. Growing up, his aunt had ingrained in all of them that she might not always be right, but she was never wrong. Truth was, she was almost always right. “Let’s knock on a few more doors and then if it’s not too late, we can stop at the café.”

“Sounds like a plan.” Joanna leaned forward, and on tippy toe, planted a soft kiss on his cheek. “Still coming to my rescue.”

All Finn could manage was half a smile. For years he and Joanna had pretended their way through different stages of coupled bliss to keep away unwanted suitors, but nowhere in the files of his mind did he find any memory of Joanna’s lips leaving him feeling warm all over. What the heck just happened?

CHAPTER EIGHT

If the citizens of Tuckers Bluff didn't have ancestors who'd once lived in one nearby now abandoned town or another, they knew someone who did. The town that intrigued her the most was Three Corners. So far Ned and the sisters were the only two from that particular ghost town. "I feel as though I've barely scratched the surface."

"Could be." Finn held the café door open for her.

It had taken a few visits to different establishments on Main Street, but Joanna had finally gotten back in the habit of waiting for Finn to reach the door first. There were so many guy friends in school who had similar manners, but years of once again living in the bigger cities and Joanna had slipped back to whoever got to the door first, opened it. Not that she couldn't open her own dang door, but the courtesy was, well, nice.

"Pick your spot," a waitress called to Finn from behind the counter.

"Keep going to the last booth on the end." His hand slid to the small of her back and ushered her forward.

Once she'd taken a step to walk ahead, his hand had fallen back to his side. The sense of loss surprised her. She was going to have to get out more when she returned home. Stop saying no to all the frogs in case one turned out to be a prince. Maybe even give in and give Peter that shot at a second date. Finn momentarily touched her once again as she slid into the booth. Then again, maybe frogs were just frogs.

The two had barely settled into their seats when Joanna looked up at the sound of the over door bell and a tall handsome man in jeans, a blue shirt, and a cowboy hat stepped into the place. "Uh." She tapped Finn's hand.

"Yeah?" Finn looked from his hand to her face.

"I could be wrong, but I think that hunk coming in our direction is another Farraday."

Finn looked over his shoulder and laughed. "Don't tell Adam you think he's a hunk. It might go to his already too big head."

"I heard that." Adam hung his hat on the hook and then gestured for his brother to move over. "Just about every one of my patients today had to tell me that you and a pretty lady are going around asking questions about ghost towns."

"We have been." Finn waved his hand from her to his brother. "Joanna, this is Adam."

"The oldest." She extended her hand to him. It had been sometime during her sophomore year when Finn had shared the story of how his siblings were all named alphabetically because of his mom's love for an old musical.

Adam nodded. "That would be me."

"And your wife owns the bed and breakfast in town?"

"Guilty again." Adam flashed a smile.

Looking from brother to brother, Joanna found herself comparing the two. So far the men she'd met had all clearly come from the same mold. The wide sincere grin clearly a staple in the Farraday genetics, but only Finn's smile reflected the twinkle in his eyes. She'd always liked his smile. From the first day they'd met in class, she'd known he was one of the nicer nice guys just from his smile.

"So tell me," Adam looked to his brother, "why in the world are you wanting to know about ghost towns?"

"That would be my fault." Joanna raised her hand near her ear and wiggled her fingers. "I'm writing an article for *Texas Travel.* I'd like some fresh background information."

Adam nodded, glanced sideways at Finn, and at Finn's single shoulder shrug, then looked back to Joanna squinting. "Joanna? Now I remember. You're one of the roommates?"

"That's right."

Finn shifted in his seat.

"Two years. Right?"

Joanna nodded. "Yep. Junior and Senior year."

Adam nodded and looked at Finn again. "Were all your roommates this smart and pretty?"

Finn rolled his eyes and Joanna felt warmth rise to her cheeks. She had a feeling the conversation not spoken between Finn and Adam was more personal than a mere compliment.

"Will Meg be joining y'all?" The waitress appeared at the tableside.

"Nah, my last appointment cancelled and I stopped in to get the scoop from the horse's mouth."

The waitress nodded. "You mean about the article?"

"You know about it?" Finn asked.

"Seriously? That's all anyone has been talking about for hours." She put her notepad in her pocket and with her right hand started counting off fingers on her left hand. "One, Joanna is not in any way related to the TV star of the same name. Two, you and she were housemates in college, not to be confused with," she made quote marks with her fingers before resuming counting off, "roommates. Three, she's writing a big magazine article about ghost towns and wants history that hasn't been written down yet. Four, everyone in town is now hunting through their attics and garages in hopes of finding something that will get them mentioned in a brief thank you paragraph that to them is as good as making it into the pages of a *New York Times* bestseller." She stopped counting and retrieved her pad and pen. "Did I forget anything?"

Finn muffled a laugh with a cough and shook his head. "Nope, sounds like you've got the key points down."

"Good. So," she looked to Joanna, "nice to meet you. Will you two be staying for dinner or is this just a hankering for Frank's pie of the day?"

Finn's gaze lifted to the chalkboard on the opposite wall. "Oh man, blackberry cobbler."

"And homemade vanilla ice cream," the waitress added.

Adam lifted his eyes to the sign, shifted his attention to the wall with a pass thru to the kitchen, then down to his watch and sucking in a breath slid out of the booth, "Better make mine to go. Two."

"Will a bit of cobbler ruin your appetite?" Finn looked to Joanna.

"Not even close. After all the walking we just did I could probably eat the whole tray."

Finn chuckled. "Why am I not surprised." He nodded at the waitress. "We'll have two also."

With a dip of her chin and a nod at Adam, the woman hurried back to the kitchen.

"She seems really nice," Joanna said.

"Abbie's the best." Adam reached for his hat. "If it wasn't for her intuition things might have turned out differently for my wife."

"Really?" Joanna followed Abbie with her eyes, taking in how efficiently the woman went from task to task. Chatting and smiling at customers as she passed or as they called to her on their way in or out of the café. "Business is pretty good here."

Adam smiled. "You might have something to do with that. But I'm going to head home and see what my wife is up to." The man's grin grew mischievously wider and once again heat flushed to Joanna's cheeks and she had to glance down to keep from grinning herself.

Adam had already retrieved his dessert and was halfway out the door when Joanna looked up at Finn. "Has anyone ever said they should make a TV movie about your family?"

"Mine?" Finn's hand flattened on his breastbone.

"All your brothers are stupid in love."

"Well," Finn shrugged. "I don't know that they'd agree with the stupid part, but yeah, they've all found their perfect match. But enough of my brother's love lives. What do you think for the story?"

"I think," Joanna flattened her palms on the table, "that Three Corners is going to be my focus. I did a quick search on my phone and couldn't find a thing. I'm sure it's the fresh angle I want. How far is it from here?"

"About an hour and half in the opposite direction of the ranch."

"Ruins? Or is it completely gone?"

"More than ruins. It's been a lot of years since I've been out that way, but I'm pretty sure most of Main Street is still intact. I know about a decade ago or so, some movie company from Dallas spruced up the façade and did some exterior shot filming out there."

"Really?" Finding the before photos would be critical for the story she wanted to tell. Or did she want to tell more than one story? If she did, that would mean spending a lot more time in the area doing research than she'd originally planned for. Taking a quick glance at Finn talking to her as if it had only been six days since they'd last seen each other and not six years, it occurred to her that having a reason to stick around might not be a bad thing at all.

• • • •

"You're Irish?" Aunt Eileen's eyes lit up and Finn knew if she got wind of the stray dog, she'd have him and Joanna walking down the aisle beside Becky and DJ.

"Fifty percent. Dad is a hodgepodge of mostly English we think, but Mom is of Irish descent and still keeps in touch with her grandmother's people in Ireland."

"Where in Ireland?" Aunt Eileen closed her knife and fork and took a slow and deliberate sip of water.

"County Cork."

Aunt Eileen lit up. "Do you know where?"

If Finn didn't know better, he'd swear his aunt's R rolled a little longer giving her Texas accent a bit of an Irish lilt.

"My mom knows, but I don't remember. I do remember my grandma was a Murphy and my Grandda was a Cotter. It's the

Murphy's that we still know in Ireland."

"Isn't that wonderful. My family is originally from County Cork. Callahan used to have a G in it. C-A-double L-A-G-H-A-N, but we lost track of our original roots generations ago."

"What about the Farradays?"

"I'm afraid," Finn's dad leaned forward at the table, "the original O'Fearadaigh has been somewhat butchered. From what Uncle George remembers my great grandfather saying, we originally hail from County Donegal, but Uncle George doesn't remember the name of the town. We assume it was too much of a mouthful for him at the time."

"Speaking of mouthfuls, who's up for dessert?" Aunt Eileen pushed away from the table and stood.

"There's always room for dessert." The Farraday patriarch patted his stomach and then stood to help his sister-in-law clear the table.

"I'm sure I can find a little room," Joanna chimed in.

When she tried to join the others in clearing the dinner dishes, Finn stuck his arm out and snatched the plate from her hands. "Guests don't clean up."

"But—"

Shaking his head at her, Ethan hobbled past her on his way to the kitchen with his own dishes and repeated, "Guests don't clean up."

Finn shrugged at her lost expression. "Stick around long enough to pay rent and you can clean up."

"Thanks." Joanna rolled her eyes at him, really pretty blue eyes.

"Here you go." Aunt Eileen set a plate of sweet potato pie in front of her and another in front of Finn.

"Thanks," Finn said at the same time as Joanna. "So," he stabbed at his pie, "what's the plan for tomorrow? Helping with the new fence?"

Reflexively, Joanna's hand slid to her hip and rubbed her thigh. "I think I'd like to drive out to Three Corners and take a look around. Take some photos for reference."

"You should go with her." Finn's dad took his seat at the table. "You never know what's wandering around empty buildings like that."

It took him all of five seconds, maybe seven to weigh the situation. Connor would be working with his horses at his own place tomorrow and would be unable to help out again. Putting up the new section of fence was more than a two-man job, which meant leaving his dad and Sam alone would just create a backlog of work. The answer was pretty easy, there was absolutely no way in hell he was letting Joanna head out to an abandoned town alone. At least not until she learned to shoot a rattler instead of climbing trees.

CHAPTER NINE

"I didn't think I'd like the peace and quiet so much." Not a morning person by nature, Joanna nodded off a time or two for the first part of the drive to Three Corners, but now she was taking in the vast distance of absolutely nothing. "And let me tell you, an empty road beats Dallas rush hours any day."

"I'm not going to argue with you. I thought College Station had too much traffic."

"Are you kidding?" Joanna sat up straighter. "I loved whipping around anywhere in town in less than ten minutes. It was great."

"You do remember it took longer than that to get to campus from our house?"

"Minor detail." Joanna shrugged a shoulder.

Head tipped back, Finn let out a rumble of laughter. "Life with you was never about the details."

"No," she smiled at him. "I suppose not."

"So remind me," he glanced her way, then back at the road in time to turn off the main drag and onto a bumpy narrow two lane road. "What teensy weensy brawl did we almost start?"

"If you don't remember, I'm not so sure I want to remind you." She really didn't want to bring up the crazy night if Finn didn't remember. She had enough antics to live down, why bring up another.

"Take a chance," he coaxed.

Boy did she wish she could skip it. "All right. It was sophomore—no wait—junior year. Fall. We'd all just moved into the house and the crew went out to celebrate our new place and Natalie's birthday."

Finn nodded. "At the Lazy Horseshoe."

"Right. See you do remember."

"The celebration, yes. The brawl, no."

"Almost brawl."

"Is that like almost pregnant?"

"Not quite." Joanna braced herself as the truck bounced over a deep pothole. "Was someone mining for gold on this road?"

"Not sure if this was originally gravel or just dirt but either way, seventy-five years of weather and heavy-hoofed cattle crossings have not been kind to it." He took his eyes off the beaten up road to pierce her with a steely blue eyed glance. "And don't change the subject. The brawl?"

"Remember the bachelor party?"

He shook his head.

"There was a bunch of guys there for a bachelor party that night. You, Chase and Pierce were playing pool, and Natalie and Calli and I were dancing and having a good time."

"The norm. Got it." He smiled at her and squeezed the steering wheel as they sailed over another bump.

"This one guy with the bachelor party kept flirting with me, or at least trying to."

"Also the norm."

Joanna did her best eye roll even if he wasn't looking. "I mostly smiled and pretended not to hear over the music."

"Sounds familiar."

"Who's telling this story?"

"Sorry." He smiled without taking his eyes off the pitted road.

"Anyhow, he finally got close enough to hit on me where I couldn't pretend not to hear him, so I told him I was with someone else."

"You could have just said no. Most of us guys are pretty much used to not every girl saying yes."

"You know I hate hurting a guy's feelings, beside the whole with-someone excuse is your fault."

"My fault?" Finn slanted a surprised glance in her direction.

"Yeah, remember? One of the first times we'd all gone as a group to the Horseshoe, that cocky football player kept hitting on me. Refused to take no for an answer."

Finn's gaze narrowed and the muscles along his jaw tightened as he bit down hard. He remembered.

"You were the only one to notice he'd backed me into the corner by the ladies room."

"And I told him to get his hands off you." Finn's knuckles whitened around the steering wheel. "I should have broken them."

"Yeah, well, when he puffed up like he was facing an opposing linebacker on the field, and said, '*who's going to stop me*?' you stared him down and said—"

"I will."

Joanna nodded. "I thought all hell was going to break loose and instead, his eyes widened, and he stepped back apologizing that he didn't realize we were together, sputtered no offense, man, and practically slithered away."

"And?" Finn prompted.

"And that's when I realized a good offense was the best defense."

She flashed her teeth in a cheeky grin that turned sincere when he chuckled and momentarily taking his eyes off the road, smiled at her.

"You, JoJo," he shook his head like a parent amused with a brazen child, "are something else."

"I'll take that as a compliment." She leaned back in her seat.

"It was meant as one. Now tell me the rest of the brawl story."

"You really want to hear this?"

Finn dipped his chin in a single affirmative nod. "I do."

"All right," she blew out a breath, "this guy was almost as bad as that stupid football player, only even having a boyfriend wasn't enough to shake him off. He wanted to know if I was hooked up, why was I alone?"

Finn blinked and Joanna knew he was retrieving that night's data from his memory banks. The whole thing was still pretty vivid in her mind.

"Hey handsome," Joanna sidled up beside Finn at the pool table and gave him a peck on the cheek.

He gave a soft chuckle and barely shifted his gaze to the dance floor behind them, sliding his arm around her waist. "So who are we scaring off this time?"

"The loudmouth drunk in the red shirt and glasses."

"I'm guessing," Finn retrieved his arm to chalk the cue tip, "you didn't try saying you weren't interested."

"If I had he's too drunk to listen."

Finn's brow furrowed as he scanned the dancefloor more carefully. "Did he do something to you?"

"No. I mean, other than patting my butt once, though he might have just been reaching for the chair and missed, and grabbing my arm when I'd try to turn away, but nothing I couldn't walk away from." She recognized the look on Finn's face. She may not be his girlfriend, fiancée, or wife for real, but she was his friend and he was very protective of her. Truth be told, he was protective of all their friends. More than once she'd seen him step up and help a girl having trouble with a drunk even when he didn't know her. Which was to Joanna's good fortune because he didn't mind being pulled in as her pretend other half to stave off the losers.

"Save that thought, it's my turn." Finn gave her a kiss on the forehead, his eyes carefully watching the crowd over her head, and stepped forward to take his shot.

She raised her thumb at him for good luck. Too bad they didn't really have a thing going. There simply wasn't a nicer guy in the state. And he wasn't bad looking either.

Natalie came up beside her. "Did you say something to that guy in the red shirt?"

"Told him I was with Finn."

"Did you tell anyone else that?"

"No, why?"

"Because he asked me if you were attached. I saw you over

here with Finn and put two and two together, but he doesn't look like the type to give up easy."

By the huge grin on Finn's face, Joanna knew he'd once again beaten Chase.

"You might as well accept it. I'm the superior player," Finn teased his friend and back at Joanna's side, his gaze once again on the crowd, he slid his arm around her waist. "I think it's time we move on."

Joanna spotted the guy in the red shirt talking to Calli. "Crap."

"What?" Finn asked.

"Nothing. I think you're right. I'll go tell Nat." At that moment Calli's face scrunched in a look of total confusion as she shook her head and Joanna knew she's been busted. "Better yet, let's get the car and I'll text Nat to meet us outside."

Finn's expression clearly said you're-up-to-something, but like the good sport he was, he escorted her outside and she frantically texted Nat to round everyone up.

"That was the night you were avoiding some drunk with glasses?"

"Right," Joanna confirmed. "I guess no one ever told you what happened as we were leaving?"

"What happened?"

"The guy in the red shirt made the rounds asking if you and I were an item. When he got to Calli, who never was good at thinking fast on her feet, she told him we were just friends. He'd come looking for us, but we'd already slipped out. Unfortunately, Chase and Pierce were still making their way to the door when the guy in the red shirt, backed up with his party, shoved Chase looking for you."

"Shit. How did I not find out about this?"

Joanna shrugged. She would have thought for sure someone would have told him the same way Nat had told her. "I don't know, but Chase of course shoved back—"

"Sounds like Chase."

"And just as some of our friends got up to even the odds, Nat, Calli and some of the Kappa girls slid between the lines, separating them. Men being men…"

"They went after the girls and Chase and Pierce—"

"Got dragged out by Calli and Nat," she finished for him. "We wound up going for something to eat and they went on to the next bar."

"And the whole almost brawl got forgotten." Finn shrugged. "Guy was a jerk anyhow."

"Yeah." She'd met a lot of those through the years. Guys seemed to be taking longer to grow up these days. "Oh look." Her arm pointed straight ahead. Sitting cockeyed to face Finn as she retold the story, she hadn't noticed how close they'd gotten to town.

"Welcome to Three Corners," Finn said.

• • • •

Joanna looked ready to leap out of the moving truck. He'd forgotten how enthusiastic she could get over just about anything. Even when she'd drag him into one of her performances for the suckers drooling over her, she put her all into it. Truth was, he'd enjoyed those little charades.

Most of the pretty blondes got all the attention on the college bar strip, but Joanna was striking even with her chestnut brown hair. Big blue eyes that changed shades from clear to brazen depending on the color clothes she wore could draw a man in with the bat of an eyelash. And Joanna batted those lashes well when she needed to. Sometimes just to make him laugh. He missed that. By the time they'd graduated, they'd gotten so good at the routine that half the campus thought they really were an item.

Slowing to a stop, Finn slid the truck into park in the middle of what should have been the main drag, and turned to Joanna. "Ready?"

"You bet." She'd already had her belt unbuckled and one foot out the door.

"It's not a race." He called to her as she scurried to the dirty window of the nearest building.

"Oh my, it's all still in there." She rubbed the window and cupped her hands around her eyes. "It's the general store."

Finn peered inside. "Sure looks like it." Though the shelves were far from fully stocked, it was easy to get an idea of what the place must have been like once upon a time.

"I can picture all the people." Joanna straightened and looked down the empty street. "A whole town." She sighed. "Here one day and gone the next."

"Funny how some towns in the middle of nowhere sprang to life while others withered away." Finn hadn't given any of it much thought through the years.

From storefront to storefront, they walked side by side, peering into windows, testing doors. Wandering inside when able.

"I wish I had a better camera." Joanna snapped a photo of a rusty old dressmaker's mannequin. "I wonder what the story was here?"

Finn had wondered the same thing. Nearing the end of the short main street, inset off the dirt road, yellow straw blowing in the wind, the front courtyard of the old church came into view.

"Oh, Finn." Her eyes grew impossibly wider. "Just like *Little House on the Prairie*. Come on." Joanna waved him forward and took off at a near gallop down the street.

Finn took off after her. "Hold up. You've gotta be—" his remaining words strangled by Joanna's ear piercing scream.

CHAPTER TEN

"Full house. Read 'em and weep." Aunt Eileen spread her cards on the table and gathered her chips. The cards had been on her side today.

Ruth Ann shook her head. "I swear if anyone touched you today they'd get burned. You and those cards are on fire."

"We are, aren't we?" Aunt Eileen couldn't help grinning. Not playing for real money, the card games were all in fun, more about fellowship than winning. But winning was still nice.

"So when do we get to meet this new houseguest of yours?" Sally May gathered the cards in front of her. "Word is she's cute as a button."

Aunt Eileen shrugged. "She's more than cute. She's beautiful. And I'm sure you'll get to meet her soon enough. I'm thinking she'll stick around until she gets to talk to everyone."

"Sissy says she's real nice too." Ruth Ann folded her hands in front of her while Sally May shuffled. "They're awfully excited about sharing their ancestry with her. They also said she and Finn make an adorable couple. "

Eileen had thought the same thing. "Hm."

"You don't look happy about it?" Sally May dealt the first card. "Is she not as nice as everyone says? You think she's got ulterior motives to showing up?"

"No. I'm sure she's here to write." Eileen sorted her first card in her hand. "I've just never seen Finn quite so…"

"Chipper?" Ruth Ann filled in.

"Happy?" Dorothy said next.

Eileen looked to her two friends. "I was going to say interested."

"Cause," Sally May dealt the last card, "word on the street is no one has ever seen Finn smiling so much as when he was taking her around town yesterday."

"Heck," Ruth Ann sorted her cards, "Ned said he wasn't sure he'd ever seen Finn look so spry."

"Spry?" Eileen tossed out two cards. "What is Finn, an old man?"

"Of course not." Dorothy looked to her friend. "All he meant is that this girl, Joanna, seems to have an impact on Finn."

That's what had Eileen feeling unsettled. It was silly of her. For years she would have danced naked to the full moon for her boys to find nice women anywhere they could. Now that five of her six boys had found the perfect matches, she was overjoyed, but worried about Finn.

"You look like you sucked on a lemon." Dorothy set her cards on the table face down. "What's going on in that little mind of yours?"

"It's silly."

"Okay," Ruth Ann said. "What's silly?"

"Adam, Brooks, Connor, DJ and Ethan are so very happy with the women in their lives."

Sally May looked up from her cards. "And that's a bad thing?"

"Of course not. It's just that each and every one of those matches was either orchestrated by, introduced by, or sanctioned by—"

"Oh, for mercy's sake, you are not going to mention that dog." Dorothy rolled her eyes at Eileen. "It's just a stray mutt. Heck, it's not even the same stray mutt."

Sally May shrugged. "Dorothy's right. Ethan saw his dog in California."

"And Adam and Meg never got a really good look at their dog." Ruth Ann set two cards aside. "You can't seriously tell me you don't want Finn to find happiness if there's no dog involved?"

"Of course not." Eileen fidgeted with her cards. She wasn't crazy. She just wished that darn dog would show up.

• • • •

Oh, God. Why hadn't she stayed in the truck? What was she thinking running loose in West Texas? Hadn't she learned her lesson the first time? Only now, there was no tree, no fence, and not more than three feet between her and the hissing rattlesnakes. Both of them.

Joanna had no clue if snakes were like bears or dogs or venomous insects. Did snakes fall under the same concept of bees, ignore them and they would ignore you or more like a bear or mama lion, disturb them and you die.

"Don't move," Finn called out. She could barely breathe, never mind move. Mere seconds passed before one and then another shot rang out.

The two deadly threats wiggled and jerked about and air slowly re-filled Joanna's lungs, but her feet remained rooted to the ground beneath her.

"JoJo, are you okay?" Finn's steady voice sounded beside her.

Without hesitation, she spun about and burying her face in his shoulder, cried out the fear.

"Hey, it's all right. They're gone." His arms folded around her, one hand swirling soothing circles against her back. "You just didn't give them time to slither away before you got close."

"I don't like snakes," she managed to mutter, her fists clenched between her shaking body and Finn's rock hard chest.

"I know this is hard to believe, but they were probably more afraid of you."

"Nuh-uh," she mumbled into his shirt. "Are they everywhere?"

"No." His hand brushed at her back. "Just in tall grasses. They like to be left alone. Usually the sound of approaching hooves or cars or even steps is enough for them to scurry away, but you bolted in so quickly you just startled them."

Her head shot up and she glared at him. "*I* startled *them*?"

A soft rumble sounded from deep in his throat. "Yes. You

did."

Her phone rang and she slid it out of her back pocket without moving away from the safety of Finn's hold and holding the phone out, clicked speaker. "Hello."

"How's it going?" Denise, the editor at *Texas Travel* who had originally tapped her for the article on the ghost towns, sounded pretty chipper.

Joanna glanced at the dead snakes. "Peachy."

"Good. Listen, I ran into a problem with my cover piece for the Winter edition. The author is getting a divorce. If you can get me your story sooner than later, the spot is yours."

"Really?" She straightened just a little. "How much sooner?"

"Two weeks should do it."

"I can do that." The cover of *Texas Travel* would be huge. Now she really needed a hooky angle and with any luck, Three Corners would do it for her.

"Great. We'll need some better pics than your camera. I'll see who I can round up that's any good on short notice. I'll need your schedule."

"Just send whoever to Tuckers Bluff. This will be home base till the piece is done."

"Good. Good. I'll keep you posted. And Joanna?"

"Yeah?"

"If this works you'll get more lead spots."

"Thanks." A few more short words and she slid the phone back into her purse.

"Sounds like good news." Finn hadn't made any effort to pull away.

"My first cover spot."

Finn's smile spread from ear to ear and she couldn't explain why it meant so much more to her that he understood this was a big deal.

"Then," Finn chucked her chin lightly with his finger, "we'd better get snooping."

"I think I've had enough for today." Her nerves steadier,

Joanna took a step back, even though she really didn't want to leave the comfort or safety of Finn's arms just yet. "I've come. I've seen. Let's just pretend I conquered."

This time Finn laughed with a little more gusto. "Done."

On the walk back to the truck, Joanna kept to the middle of the road and ran her options for the story around in her head. When her thoughts circled back to the snakes, she stopped and turned to face Finn at her side. "Do you always carry a gun?"

He shook his head. "No. This isn't the Wild West. But when I know I'm going to be out walking in prime rattler napping ground. Yeah. I do."

"You had a rifle on the four by four."

He nodded. "You never know what you're going to run into on a hundred thousand acres of cow country. It's just smart."

This time she nodded, took a few steps and stopped again to look up at him. "Can you teach me?"

"To shoot?" One brow arched high on his forehead. Another thing he did that she'd forgotten how cute it made him look.

"Yes."

"Why?"

"I don't know. Would I be correct if I said your aunt knows how to shoot a gun?"

His head bobbed up and down. "Every person on a ranch knows how to safely handle a fire arm."

"So would you say all the women who lived in this town knew how to handle a gun?"

He hesitated. "Probably not. For these folks this was a city. The women counted on the men and the law to handle the guns."

"So, what you're saying is it's a need for the rancher way of life not city life?"

"Yeah, I guess that's what I'm saying."

"I'd like to learn."

His gaze lingered over her shoulder in the distance for a few long seconds before he blew out a heavy breath and nodded. "All right. We can do that."

Joanna smiled. Not that she ever expected to need a gun in Dallas, but the idea of understanding more of Finn's world and fitting in like she had yesterday morning made her want to grin as though she'd won Powerball.

• • • •

Today was not turning out to be anything like Finn had expected. For starters, he actually had been enjoying bopping down the sidewalk of Three Corners, peeking in windows and poking around inside the abandoned shops and offices. Joanna had been overly silly with the camera on her phone. For Finn, his phone was all about answer and hang up. A way to communicate. The word selfie was not part of his vocabulary.

And yet, he'd been a party to what had to be a hundred crazy shots of him and Joanna at the dress shop, the general store, the restaurant, even the saloon. She'd stood on one foot, leaned forward, leaned back, kissed him on the cheek, stuck her fingers in her ears and made ridiculous faces, and he hadn't laughed so hard in years.

But the sight of Joanna paralyzed in fear with a pair of rattlers practically at her feet had his blood pumping hard. Though not nearly as hard as it had flowed when she'd collapsed into his arms. He couldn't count all the times they'd danced together, hugged hello, goodbye, or held each other to ward off an unwanted suitor, but he knew for sure not once had having her body mold to his sent his mind running free with thoughts he had no right to dwell on.

Now she wanted to learn to shoot a gun. To do what his aunt did and just about every woman within a few hundred miles of Tuckers Bluff could do. A small part of him thought putting a gun with live ammo in Joanna's hands was not the brightest move he'd ever make, but another side was damn pleased that she wanted to ride horses, mend fences, and shoot guns. It made no bloody sense. None of it did. But it was what it was, and he had no idea what to do about any of it.

CHAPTER ELEVEN

Bringing the knife down on the tail end of the celery, Joanna scraped the last bits into the bowl. “Celery minced. Now what?”

Aunt Eileen waved her own knife at Joanna. “Pour them into the pan with the mushrooms and give them a good stir.”

“Got it.” Joanna did as she was told, mixing in the diced veggies and sautéing them in the butter. “This smells wonderful.”

“On the days I play cards in town, I always make something fast and easy. If I’m back too late there are a gazillion frozen casseroles in the utility room freezer.”

“My mom used to do that. Save casseroles for a rainy day. Never failed when she ran out of room in the freezer, she’d invite the neighbors and we’d have a smorgasbord for dinner.”

“Sounds nice.” Aunt Eileen continued mashing the potatoes.

“It was.” Joanna lifted the lid on the back pot and noticing the sauce boiling too hard, lowered the flame and replaced the lid.

“So you like to cook?” Aunt Eileen watched Joanna out of the corner of her eye.

Joanna shrugged. “Don’t know that I’d say I like to cook, but I don’t dislike cooking.”

“But you know how to cook. I have two nieces-in-law who wouldn’t have had a clue to check on the sauce.”

“Let me guess, Catherine?”

Aunt Eileen nodded. “Not much time in law school for cooking classes.”

“And,” Joanna had to think a second, “Becky and DJ aren’t married yet, and every New England Italian I ever met knows at least a little something about cooking so I’d guess it’s not Toni.”

“Nope. Not Toni.”

"That leaves Meg the innkeeper and … wait, is Ethan married?"

"Not yet."

"Then you can't be referring to Allison, so it must be Meg. But she runs a bed and breakfast?"

Aunt Eileen laughed. "Yep. She can scramble eggs and fry bacon and Toni supplies all the baked goods. Toni's blueberry muffins are popular. If the place were a bed and supper, Meg would be screwed."

Joanna almost choked on her own spit. She hadn't expected sweet Aunt Eileen to say that. "Uh, I guess."

"Oh, that smells good." Catherine, the niece-in-law who wasn't much of a cook, came in the front door. "Are you making that creamy shepherd pie thing?"

Aunt Eileen nodded. "I am, and there's plenty if your crew wants to join us."

"Thanks, but Connor's up to his eyeballs in some new designs for the corrals and Stacey is on a cream cheese and jelly sandwich kick."

"Oh." Aunt Eileen beamed. "I made that for our lunch the other day."

"Well, it's safe to say, like everything else the two of you do, it was a big hit." Catherine turned to Joanna. "The reason I popped over is to invite you to join some of us girls' tonight."

"Tonight?"

Catherine nodded. "A bunch of us go out around once a month on a Friday night just to get away. Tonight Kelly is a little under the weather over some idiot she just broke up with."

"Not that new fella she seemed to like?" Aunt Eileen flashed an irritated scowl.

"Yep." Catherine bobbed her head. "He kept fussing at her about her eating and her weight. Finally told her she could stand to lose a few pounds."

"She's got a nice full figure." Aunt Eileen's gaze flashed so cold and hard that Joanna almost took a step back. "One a *real* man would appreciate."

Catherine's hands went up palm out. "Don't tell me. You're preaching to the choir. Anyhow," she looked to Joanna again, "we all thought a drive out to Butler Springs and the Boot 'N' Scoots was in order. You up to it?"

"Oh, I don't—"

"Go on and say yes." Aunt Eileen's frown disappeared. "You'll have fun. Music is good for the soul. And the imagination."

"I suppose if Finn doesn't mind."

"Mind what?" Finn walked in the door as if he'd been summoned.

"If she joins us for girls' night," Catherine answered.

Finn shrugged and smiled. "That's up to you. I'm probably going to turn out the lights early tonight anyhow."

"Well." She did like the idea of getting to know everyone better. "Yes. Thank you."

"Great. I've got the truck out front. Meg's expecting us."

"Oh. I should probably change."

"Nope. We don't stand on formality around here." Catherine smiled, turned to Aunt Eileen and kissed her on the cheek. "Save me some of that, please. It'll be great for lunch."

"You bet." Aunt Eileen nodded.

"Will I need a key?" Joanna grabbed her purse. "Or will someone be up?"

"No need for a key." Finn grabbed a biscuit from the breadbasket. "Not much need for locks around here."

"Oh. Then, guess I'll see you later." With a wave and a smile, Joanna followed Catherine out the door. Life in West Texas sure was unpredictable. Rattling snakes in the morning and boot scooting at night.

• • • •

Only two previous nights spent with Joanna joining the family at the dinner table and something didn't feel right not having her here tonight. Finn was definitely losing it. She was an old college pal. A good friend, but nothing more. He definitely needed to get out more. Not spend what little off time he had on the ranch. At least once in a while.

"Don't you think?" his father said.

Finn had no idea what was being discussed at the table. "I'm sorry, think what?"

"That Jake Thomas and his wife are better off with her people?"

"Oh, well." Finn hadn't given much thought to it, but old man Thomas was definitely not one of the most supportive people in the world.

"I think it's important that he know the town doesn't hold him responsible for what happened." Aunt Eileen picked at her food with the edge of her fork. "The poor man was sick. "

"Anything new on the case?" Ethan gave his daughter a Cheerio and her swing a nudge.

"According to DJ," their father said, "with the additional information from the specialist on brain tumors that Allison recommended, the judge has finally agreed to interim probation with medical evaluations and monitoring of behavior to determine if the tumor was indeed the cause of his dangerous behavior. Jake Sr. says Jake Jr. and his wife are going to settle permanently near Houston."

"I still can't stand the idea that Jake Jr. doesn't feel he can come back here." Aunt Eileen pushed to her feet and lifted her empty dish and silverware. "Though I am glad that the doctor's feel he'll make a full recovery and will be back to his old friendly self."

Finn's phone buzzed in his pocket. He didn't get many personal calls but tonight he was especially glad to hear it ring.

"Excuse me." He lifted a finger and walking his plate from the dining room to the kitchen sink, answered his phone. "Hello."

"You got plans tonight?" Reed Taylor, one of the patrol

officers under DJ, asked without introduction. "Ken Brady and I are thinking of heading to Butler Springs for a little Friday night R and R."

The invitations to join his childhood friends had been coming fewer and farther apart. The usual, 'no thanks, I'm beat,' was about to spill from his lips when he remembered not ten minutes ago he'd told himself he needed to get out more. "Free as a bird. What's the plan?"

"Probably Delancey's. Grab a couple of beers. Watch a game on any of a dozen screens. Maybe shoot some pool."

"Sounds good to me. Be at your place in an hour."

"Great. See ya then."

Twenty minutes later he was well on his way when his phone rang again. This time it was Ken. "Listen, my car doesn't want to turn over and it won't take a jump. You mind swinging out my way and picking me up?"

"No problem." Fortunately, Finn hadn't reached the turn off yet for Ken's place. A century ago the dirt drive had been the entry to a single ranch. Through the decades the land had been parceled out by varying acres to the expanding family. Some folks had more land than others. Some merely owned a house on a decent plot off the main drag, known as Brady Road, for the last generation or so.

At the far end of the road, Ken still had his head under the hood when Finn's quad cab rumbled up. Ken slammed the hood shut and shaking his head, grabbed a nearby rag, wiped his hands, tossed it aside, and climbed into the truck.

"You look pretty neat for someone who just had their head in an engine." Finn shifted the engine into drive.

"Just looking, not touching. It's gotta be the starter."

"Sure it's not the alternator?"

Ken shook his head. "Not sure of anything. I'm better with four hooves than four wheels."

"I hear you." Finn had to laugh. He knew enough about cars to keep them from throwing a rod from lack of oil, but that was about all he knew. Ethan and Connor were the mechanically inclined of the family.

"Man, I am so ready to get out and away from all things cow."

Again, Finn chuckled with his friend. He loved what he did, but Ken was right. Between his brothers all pairing up, children joining the family, new babies on the way, and now Joanna around to make him smile, Finn realized there was a very good reason why people for centuries had been maligning all work and no play. He definitely needed to play.

Finn had no idea how they'd gone from the plan of a few beers and a game on the big screen to pulling up to the Boots 'N' Scoots, but here they were.

"Surely Tuckers Bluff has grown enough to warrant having its own little night spot?" Ken climbed out of the backseat of the truck.

Reed slammed his door shut. "The problem is we're one of the few all dry counties in the state. There just isn't enough interest to make Tuckers Bluff wet."

"Has anyone ever tried?" Ken asked, looking to Finn then Reed.

Finn shrugged. Driving an hour into his hometown at the end of a workday for a beer held little appeal. Though driving into Tuckers Bluff on a Friday night made a lot more sense than hauling ass ninety miles to Butler Springs.

"Maybe," Ken followed Reed and Finn inside, "it's time our generation brought it up again."

"Okay," Reed stepped aside, "let's say the town votes to make Tuckers Bluff wet. Who's going to invest in a night time establishment when half the neighboring residents don't actually live in town?"

"Think of it as a baseball movie. If we build it, they will come." And with a huge face-splitting grin, Ken marched to the bar.

Reed shook his head and turned to Finn. "The thing is, it's not a half bad idea if you can get the liquor thing past the blue haired church ladies."

Visions of his aunt and her card-playing friends along with a wall of empty booze bottles in the kitchen flashed in front of Finn. "I have a feeling the tide may be turning on that one."

The two of them had barely caught up with Ken at the bar when a pretty brunette caught his eye and he was off to dance.

"He was right. A little dance time with the ladies is good for what ails a man." Finn surveyed the crowded dance hall and then his brows dipped into a mini-frown. "Hell."

"What?" Finn followed his direction and spotted the table in question. "I thought they were going to Meg's?"

"I didn't think about girls-Friday-night-out at all." Reed expelled a long breath "No matter. It's not like any of us were planning on making an all-nighter out of this."

"Agreed. Might as well say hello." Finn led the way. Though the original reason for tagging along with his friends had been to get out and shake his thoughts clear of Joanna, as the table of town women grew closer, he found himself just more than a little pleased to have wound up at the same place as her.

"Well aren't you all a sight for sore eyes." The latest addition to the girls night out gang, a Marilyn Monroe wanna-be since childhood, jumped to her feet and quickly sidled up to Reed. Finn wondered how much of the sweet dumb blonde was real and how much was an act. "Care to dance with little old me?"

Like the gentleman that would make any parent proud, Reed extended his elbow and smiled down. "It would be my pleasure."

They squirmed their way through the crowds, leaving Finn the only man standing at a table of nothing but smiling women. He tried not to let his gaze shift too quickly to Joanna, but the effort was futile, her fingers tapped in rhythm with her toes and the tune blaring in the background. "Shall we take a turn?" He extended his hand to her.

"Thought you'd never ask."

CHAPTER TWELVE

"I just love this song." Becky swayed in her seat to the tune of "I Like the Sound of That" and turned to the rest of the girls seated at the table with her. "I'm thinking we need to start doing a dancing date night once a month, too."

"Oh." Drumming her fingers on the table in time with the music, Catherine nodded. "Even I can two-step."

"So is this just for the married people?" Kelly, Adam's receptionist, tapped her foot to the beat.

"Nope." Becky wished that DJ were here now so they could do a twirl on the floor. For years coming here on girls' night every so often had been a lot of fun, but tonight it just didn't feel the same anymore. "Anyone can come and bring a date or find a date."

Meg gave a thumbs-up. "I like the idea. Good to get out of town and have a nice dinner and then do a little boot scootin'."

"Boot scootin'?" Toni chuckled. "Saints preserve us, we've become Texans."

"Speak for yourself." Meg waved a finger. "I've always been a Texan."

"Yeah," Toni nodded. "But a city Texan. Did you even know how to two-step before you married Adam?"

"Well," Meg's cheeks turned a rosy shade, "I didn't know a lot about living before marrying Adam."

"I'll say one thing for sure." Toni casually waved a finger at the dance floor. "For a city girl, Joanna seems to scoot her boots just fine."

"I'd scoot my boots just fine too if I were dancing with a Farraday." Kelly glanced up at the multiple sets of eyes that had turned in her direction. "None of your Farradays of course."

The table rumbled with laughter and Meg shifted her attention to the dance floor. “They do look a bit cozy.”

Two steps forward and a shuffle back, Finn and Joanna followed the circle of dancers around the dance floor and at the moment Meg looked up, Finn gave his partner a little twirl and Joanna burst into giggles.

“This is certainly not the first time they’ve been dancing.” Catherine focused on the couple. “There seems to be quite an air of familiarity between them.”

“The question,” Meg kept her gaze on the dancing duo, “is how familiar?”

“Do you think back in college they had more of a horizontal tango going on?” Toni asked.

Both Becky and Kelly whipped their heads around to face Toni as if she’d asked if Finn had participated in sacrificing a virgin to the volcano gods. The idea was almost laughable. Becky shook her head. “Have you learned nothing about the Farraday men?”

Kelly blew out a sigh. “Dogs don’t crap where they eat and the Farradays don’t play around with friends. If Finn and she shared a house with friends, you can bet your last dollar he never laid a hand on her.” She cleared her throat. “At least not, well… you know what I mean.”

“The Farradays do all seem to have an unusually wide honor streak,” Toni agreed.

“A bit old fashioned.” Catherine smiled. “Kinda nice.”

All the women returned their attention to the couple on the dance floor. Another spin and turn, a laugh, and when the chorus came about “too loud on the highway” Finn’s lips seemed to move in time with the lyrics.

“Is he singing to her?” Meg leaned forward and like a crowd at a sporting event, so did the two women on either side of her.

“Looks like it, doesn’t it?” Kelly was the first to lean back in her seat. “But it is a catchy tune.”

“She’s right.” Becky turned and lifted her glass. “I’m also singing a little louder when they get to the end of a sentence and sing 'youuuuuuuu'. Makes me smile."

"I like the line about laughing too much to sleeeeeeep." Meg smiled. "Reminds me of Adam."

"I bet." Toni set her hand on her stomach and reached for her ginger ale. "We are awfully lucky. All of us."

"Too bad there aren't more brothers." Kelly hefted a lazy shoulder. "Then again, except for Becky here, the Farradays never paid much attention to the women in their own backyard. Which is why we know that if Finn says he and Joanna were just friends—"

"They were just friends," Meg and Toni repeated.

"Hell, they didn't pay much attention to me either," Becky said. "Took a baby and court ordered foster care to get their attention."

"I don't know about that." Meg tipped her head. "I always thought DJ looked at you with a little too much interest."

"Really?" Toni asked. "I thought he had something going with Abbie."

"You too?" Catherine leaned into the table to say something and then noticing the slight frown settling on Becky's face, straightened in her seat. "The important thing is DJ's head over boot-heels in love with Becky and champing at the bit for this big bash wedding to be over."

The tension in Becky's shoulders eased. "I can't believe a few more weeks and I'll be an official Farraday."

"Look." Toni pointed to the floor again. A new song came on, a little slower, and neither Finn nor Joanna showed any sign of taking a break. Toni turned to the women and lowered her voice. "Are you sure about Finn and Joanna?"

Meg and Catherine squinted their eyes, but like Becky, Kelly bobbed her head vehemently.

"One round of fresh drinks." Reed Taylor set down a glass in front of Meg, Becky and Catherine.

"That was really nice of you." Meg lifted her white wine. "You seriously didn't have to go get this."

Reed did that casual manly shrug thing and smiled. "My

pleasure. The place is packed and they don't have enough waitresses working the tables."

Once he and the Marilyn Monroe look-alike had come back from a single song spin on the dance floor, Reed realized the ladies were still waiting on re-fills of the drinks. As if his day job were bartending instead of patrolling the city streets, he'd taken the orders and disappeared into the crowd.

"Now that you've prevented these ladies from dying of thirst," Kelly stood up, "any interest in taking another turn on the dance floor?"

Reed extended his elbow as he'd done earlier. "With you, always."

They'd made it just close enough to the dance floor to be out of earshot when Toni turned to Becky. "Did I miss something with Kelly and Reed? Not that a little manly attention right now isn't what she needs, but that sounded a bit more than polite."

Becky shook her head. "Nope."

"You sure?"

"Yep. The problem with finding a good man in Tuckers Bluff is everyone has known each other since they were in diapers and it's kinda hard to think of each other as anything other than a good buddy."

Toni laughed. "Looks like a lot of friendly dancing going on for a bunch of good buddies."

Becky glanced from where Reed and Kelly joined the circle of dancers to Finn and Joanna. Where Kelly and Reed shuffled forward and back and smiled, every so often Finn leaned forward to say something to Joanna, or she leaned in to speak with him, and each time they laughed just a little harder or the smiles grew a bit wider. Either way, Becky resisted the urge to look over her shoulder and see if maybe the disc jockey was a shaggy stray dog.

• • • •

It had been way too long since Joanna had found herself on the dance floor, never mind with a man who could dance. Of all her friends in school just about everyone could do a two step, but Finn could dance. He didn't just follow the line, he twirled and spun and she absolutely loved it.

What she loved even more was the warmth of his hand at the small of her back and the strength of his other hand gently enfolding her own. "I've missed this."

"Dancing?" Finn twirled her and spun her back into the fold of his arms.

She nodded. "None of the guys I've dated over the years have done anything more than sway from side to side and too often not even to the rhythm of the music."

"Can't be that bad." Finn offered a lazy smile that sent goosebumps down her arms.

Joanna noticed just about everyone around them was moving and keeping time without any effort. "Maybe it's a country thing."

Finn's head tipped back at an eruption of laughter. "The music or the people?"

A shy smile pulled at her lips. "I suppose both."

"I don't know about all country people, but we were raised with music in the background. Once a month there's a potluck lunch at the church and there was always a fiddle and a song and a circle of dancers. We all pretty much learned to dance at the same time we learned to walk."

"I believe you." She could picture a little version of Finn dancing with his aunt in a barn with hay piled around like an old movie musical. The next song shifted the beat. A slower ballad. The circle of dancers continued to move in the same general direction, but Joanna had instinctively inched closer and to her surprise, Finn had done the same. He moved so close to her she could feel the warmth of his breath blowing lightly on her cheek.

"You look too serious. A penny for your thoughts."

No way in hell she was telling him that she liked being in his arms a little more than she should. Finn was one friend she did not want to lose. "I guess my mind wandered off to the ghost town and the story."

"Gee thanks. Nice to know when a guy is dancing with a girl, her mind is on her job."

"No." She smacked him lightly on the shoulder. "After seeing the buildings for myself I'm anxious to get my hands on the information the sisters have. I tried Googling the town name and found very little."

"Anything useful?"

"Just a few references to births and deaths, very little on the town itself. I guess the curiosity of it just tickles my mind all the time until I figure out the puzzle."

Finn chuckled. "If anyone can put the pieces together, it's you."

"Appreciate the vote of confidence."

"You know I've always been on your side."

Yes, he had. Every up and down the years she'd known him, he'd either cheered her on or held her up. Why in heaven's name had she let time and distance slip between them?

• • • •

"The crack of dawn is going to come too dang early tomorrow," Ken leaned his head back and closed his eyes.

Finn knew exactly what he meant. Any other Friday night and he'd have been all for going home over an hour ago. Even though he knew darn well that his sisters-in-law and their friends occasionally came to Boots 'N' Scoots for their traditional girls night, and even though he knew they'd gotten home without incident every single time on their own, he still couldn't bring himself to leave them in Butler Springs to drive back home alone. Fortunately, the good thing about having a police officer for a good buddy was that leaving the ladies in the bar rubbed Reed the wrong way too. "It was a good night."

Ken's lips tipped up in a sly grin. "Yeah, it was."

"How many women did you dance with?" Reed looked over

his shoulder into the backseat at his friend.

The guy shrugged and kept his eyes closed. “Lost count.”

“You seemed awfully cozy with the redhead.” Finn watched Ken in the rearview mirror.

“She was nice, but I think she was trying to shake off an ex or something, ‘cause she started getting awfully clingy. Even when I said all I wanted to do was dance.”

Finn knew what he meant. Not that he didn’t like doing the horizontal tango as much as any other red-blooded man, but sometimes all a guy wants is to have some serious fun. He felt the corners of his mouth tip up in a grin to match the one still plastered on Ken’s face. Finn couldn’t remember the last time he’d laughed so hard, or danced so long. At least not before Joanna’s arrival. And what the hell was he going to do about that? More than once he’d been too tempted to lean a fraction closer, turn his mouth a smidgen more in her direction, and taste those lips for real. But he knew too many folks that mixed friends and benefits and it hadn’t work out the way they’d pretended. Not to mention the challenges of mixing city and country. Two fast ways to kill a friendship, and much to his own surprise, Finn had no doubt that this time he didn’t want to lose his friend.

CHAPTER THIRTEEN

Almost nine o'clock. Joanna hadn't meant to sleep in, but it had been a very long time since she'd closed down a bar. Come to think of it, she wasn't sure she'd ever actually closed down a bar.

"You're moving better." Aunt Eileen held out a cup of steaming coffee. "I heard you coming down the stairs. Your stride is smoother."

"Yes, thank you. I need to remember not to wait more than a decade to ride a horse again. I may have to visit Finn more often." She wasn't sure but Aunt Eileen's smile seemed to slip just a pinch before falling back into place. What had she said? Blowing over the rim of the cup, she glanced around the kitchen and into the living room.

"The men are off working on the new fences already." Aunt Eileen opened the oven and pulled out a foil-covered dish. "I've kept the french toast casserole warm."

"Oh my, that smells divine."

Aunt Eileen's eyes twinkled brightly as her smile widened. Setting the plate down in front of Joanna, she stepped back. "The boys love it."

Stabbing at the softened bread with a fork, Joanna speared a piece and almost melted into the chair as the warm flavors burst in her mouth. "Oh, wow." She waved an empty fork. "This is so worth the calories."

"Would you like scrambled or fried eggs to go with that?"

"Nothing, please. I need to fit in my jeans when I leave."

"Nonsense." Aunt Eileen waved a spatula. "Protein isn't fattening."

"It's not the protein I'm worried about." Joanna savored

another morsel. “This is seriously way better than regular french toast.”

“Glad you like it.” Aunt Eileen slid into the seat across from her. “So, what are your plans for the day?”

“Is there a local library or newspaper?”

Aunt Eileen nodded. “Both. Why?”

“I thought I might find something on Three Corners.”

“Aren’t Sissy and Sister going to help you?”

“Oh they are, but I’m having a hard time finding facts online and thought perhaps the archives at a nearby library or paper might have something I can use.”

“I’m going into to town for my Saturday social club meeting, I’d be happy to give you a ride. Introduce you to Marion at the library.”

Joanna’s mind stuttered a second expecting Aunt Eileen to break into the song from the old musical before her thoughts caught up with what the woman was saying.

“She’s only there a few days a week,” Aunt Eileen continued, “not sure about Felix. He only puts the paper out once a week. Guess I never paid attention to the hours he keeps.”

“A ride and introduction would be wonderful.” She couldn’t decide if Felix was a thousand-year-old man who still used turn of the century typesetting or a part-time twenty something hunk whose parents had miserable taste in names. “What time are you leaving?”

“Any minute.”

“Oh.” Joanna stood. “I’ll get my laptop and my boots and meet you back here in a second.”

“Sounds like a plan.”

Joanna hurried back upstairs and exchanged her fuzzy red slippers for her borrowed boots. She’d told Finn the partial truth last night. Ever since walking the wooden sidewalks, she could feel the life of that old town in her bones and was damned anxious to find out all she could. There had to be something big worth writing about. There just had to be.

• • • •

Poker. Of all the things Joanna would have expected the ladies social club to do, playing cards would not have been even a footnote. And yet, why was she surprised? Aunt Eileen was a hoot. Probably a card shark too. She'd dropped Joanna off at the Tuckers Bluff public library and hurried on to her weekly game at the café.

Standing in the old brick building, Joanna took in the surroundings. Unlike her movie counterpart of the same name, the librarian Marion was an older woman who made the sisters look like spring chickens. Aunt Eileen had explained that the only way for the town to keep the library going was to have volunteer staff. Marion had been in charge ever since she retired from the Butler Springs public library well over ten years ago.

The woman knew every nook and cranny and had led Joanna to a dusty section of the back storage facility. "We'd been working backwards from most recent to the beginning of time to record all the data on microfiche. Now it's all about computers. Bottom line, what little we have on Three Corners is at the back of a long line to be scanned and stored."

Joanna wasn't sure if the sweet old lady was using the royal 'we' or if there really were other people to help her scan and store this stuff. Looking at the aisles of shelves filled with books and ledgers and stacks of mismatched tomes, it struck her that it might take the lifetimes of several volunteers to get it all scanned to computer. "I can take it from here."

"Oh no." Marion pulled out a pair of white cotton gloves and handed them to Joanna, then retrieved another pair for herself. "Some of these books are quite valuable. It may not look it, but this storage space is temperature controlled."

"Of course." What more could Joanna say? That the place looked like her Aunt Peggy's spare junk room? Or a scene from a Vincent Price film noir? A dangerous place to be in the dark.

"Now." Marion surveyed the printed cards on the rim of the

shelves. "I'm pretty sure we can find some of what you want…here." She came to an abrupt stop and grinning like a kid about to sit on Santa's lap, pulled out a large bound volume that Joanna assumed had to be old newspapers.

Prepared with her gloves on, Joanna received the old book, arms out, and waited as Marion continued to stack several more volumes on.

"All right. That should get us started."

An hour later a group of young teen girls had come in to use the computers for their own research project. Assured that Joanna could be trusted not to damage the old papers, Marion had delightedly hurried off to tend to the teens. It had never occurred to Joanna that there was someplace in this state where every kid didn't have their own computer, but what she found more interesting still was that not a single one seemed to mind. They'd come in laughing and giggling and gathering books before sitting down to the computer.

For the few minutes she watched the girls, Joanna felt like she'd turned on an old movie set in a simpler time. She had to ask herself who had it right, these kids or the ones back home glued to their phones.

She'd gone through volume after volume in search of anything on Three Corners. All she had uncovered was the town had, at some point, some sort of paper of their own as she found two copies of the *Three Corners Gazette*. One proudly announced the opening of the Three Corners Emporium and another with a lead article on the new cook at Millie's Restaurant. She had found a very brief piece on the arrival of God at Three Corners with the building of the new church. Most likely the one now home to her rattler friends.

In another tome filled with mostly larger town papers she'd been intrigued with the unique ads encouraging the military and university students to dine and dally in a town called Sadieville. Apparently the mayor staunchly believed in encouraging tourism to their little corner of West Texas. Joanna wasn't completely sure what made Sadieville worth the visit, but she made a mental note to look up whatever had become of the town and even took the time to snap a couple of pictures of the ads with her phone. If by chance the place had been left for dust like so many other towns in the county, it could be interesting to add it to her list.

"I see you're still here?" Aunt Eileen sneezed and rubbed her hand under her nose.

"It's a little dusty." Joanna didn't know why she felt responsible. It wasn't her job to dust the shelves.

"A little?" Aunt Eileen shook her head and came to a stop behind Joanna. "The ladies were thinking you'd been locked up here long enough and should join us for a bite to eat."

"How nice of you, but you didn't have to come all the way here for that. You could have called me."

Aunt Eileen tipped her head slightly, still smiling, but didn't say a word.

"That is," Joanna blew out a long breath and shook her head, "if I'd given you my number."

This time Aunt Eileen chuckled. "It's not that far a walk. My luck needed changing. Besides, now I've burned enough calories to have a good excuse for eating some of Frank's apple crumb pie." She leaned in, looked around as though checking for spies, and lowering her voice, said, "His is better than mine, but don't tell anyone I said that."

"No, ma'am," Joanna said.

"Smart girl. Repeat that and I'll swear in court you're lying."

Joanna laughed softly all the way back to the café. A hoot didn't even begin to cover describing Aunt Eileen.

• • • •

"If you hammer that post in any deeper it's going to pop out somewhere in China."

Finn looked from his dad to the post he was banging away on. Maybe he was a tad out of sorts. "I'm done."

"I bet." His father smiled. "Want to tell me what has you so distracted today?"

"Not distracted, just didn't get enough sleep."

"Ah." Sean Farraday bobbed his head. "Yes, well, there is a reason we ranchers tend to head to bed early."

The old cliché had been part of the Farraday mantra—early to bed, early to rise, makes a man healthy, wealthy and wise. His mom's sayings were repeated often too, even though Finn wasn't old enough to remember her saying things like, *Contemplating the immortality of the crab*, or *Repeat that and I'll swear you're lying*. Hearing either of those always brought his mother to mind. "Do you still miss her?"

Instantly, a faraway look took over the Farraday patriarch's face. He didn't need to ask who Finn meant. "Not the way you're asking. I got over that hurt a very long time ago."

"Then what?" Finn needed something to do with his hands and gave the new post an extra whack for good measure.

"When I hear Grace laugh and swear it's your mother in the room, I wish Helen were here to see how sweet our Grace of God turned out."

Finn had almost forgotten that Grace was to be Gavin. Only when she popped out a girl and his mom had said it was by the grace of God she'd had a daughter, that Grace became the next Farraday name in the alphabet.

"Same thing with you six brothers. I know how proud she'd be to see each of you grown into fine men. Each and every one of you were her pride and joy from the moment you took your first breaths. I'm always glad she got an inkling of what Adam and Brooks's lives would most likely become. It was pretty obvious that they had a lifetime passion even at ten and twelve. The veterinarian and doctor. She worried about Connor though."

"And you wonder why?" Finn picked up the scattered tools and carried them to the next post hole. Connor and Ethan were the two wild men in the family.

Sean shook his head. "Can't say I wasn't glad your mother

didn't have to worry through sleepless nights about Connor working the oil rigs. Though your Aunt Eileen did enough of that for all of us."

"That she did. I always think of Aunt Eileen as the sunny side of life. The optimist. But since Connor married Catherine and Ethan is determined to finish his time in the marines at a desk job once he's fit for duty again, Aunt Eileen has given a whole new meaning to cheery."

"You thinking about making some changes of your own?" His father set the next post into the hole. "Maybe taking dating a bit more seriously?"

Finn's gaze shot up to his father. Judging by the chuckle that erupted from deep in his dad's throat, Finn must have looked surprised as hell.

"What, son? You don't think I remember what it was like to be a young man working this ranch six days a week with nothing to keep me warm at night but some liniment?"

"Well, no. I mean, I didn't, I wasn't thinking about that." Or maybe he was—just a little. At least since Joanna had shown up. Until now, as happy as he was for his brothers, he hadn't thought he needed anything more in his life. Hadn't felt alone. Now, even with a room full of people, maybe he did. Hell, he didn't know what to think anymore.

Still smiling, his dad steadied the pole for Finn to hammer in. "The right woman has a funny way about making a man change his thinking. That is, if he was thinking at all."

Finn slammed the sledge hammer onto the post head. Maybe that was Finn's problem, maybe he should just stop thinking.

CHAPTER FOURTEEN

"Check out the suit. Three o'clock." Aunt Eileen held her cards close to her chest, her face forward, but her gaze to her right. "Citee booy."

The rest of the ladies at the table shifted in place, coughed, rubbed their neck, and performed a few other ingenious moves to inconspicuously catch a glimpse of the man who had just walked into the café.

Being an out of towner herself, Joanna had to agree with Aunt Eileen. This guy stuck out like a cactus in a rose garden. Or perhaps it was the other way around, a rose bush in a cactus patch.

"Oh, my." Sally May waved her fingers under her chin. "Not bad. Not bad at all."

"Oh for heaven's sake woman, put your eyes back in your head." Ruth Ann shook her head.

Aunt Eileen squinted at her friend. "Ruth Ann, put your glasses on."

Shooting Aunt Eileen a brief roll of her eyes, Ruth Ann set her cards face down on the table and pulled a pair of glasses from her bag. The second the spectacles were settled on the bridge of her nose, she waved her hand, fanning herself as Sally May had done. "Oh yes." Taking off the glasses, she closed the ears and put them back in her bag. "I do think I could use a fresh glass of iced tea. Extra ice."

"He sure is a cool drink, I'll give you that." Dorothy Wilson returned her full attention to the cards in front of her. "Wonder if he's passing through?"

"Probably," Nora the nurse said softly, "I wouldn't be lucky enough to have the likes of him sticking around. Especially if he's single."

"Who passes through this town all gussied up like that?" Aunt Eileen glanced from Nora to the man seated in a booth close enough to watch but far enough away to be out of ear shot and back.

"Sure looks like an expensive suit." Sally May rearranged her cards. Joanna wasn't sure but it looked like she'd just moved the same card left, then right, then left again.

"Think he's a friend of Meg's?" Ruth Ann looked to Aunt Eileen. "After all she was dressed pretty sharp first time she came into town."

Aunt Eileen pressed her lips together, shook her head and pulled out her cell. "Meg didn't say anything." Her fingers flew across the screen and a few seconds later the phone dinged and she her head "Nope. Meg doesn't have any friends coming to town, but she's on her way over."

"Oh, heavens," Sally May looked up, her eyes wide, her mouth slightly open. "You don't think he's one of Toni's, you know, first husband's kin?"

"Oh no." Ruth Ann looked to the man, then waved Abbie over.

"I was just on my way to check if you ladies needed a refill." Abbie leaned in close and forward, lowering her voice. "Our guest is waiting on old man Thomas."

All heads shifted to look at the visitor one more time before leaning back in toward Abbie.

"He didn't have much else to say," Abbie continued, "but according to Burt Larson this guy was at the feed store a good long time. Walked all around it a few times too."

"The feed store," Aunt Eileen mumbled. "Guess things really are moving forward."

Joanna looked at all the serious faces. "Who's Burt Larson?"

"Owns the hardware store," Abbie answered.

"Worse gossip than any woman in town," Ruth Ann added.

Joanna lowered her voice. "He's here?"

"Oh, no." Abbie grinned. "He phoned in. Always does when

he sees something interesting going on. He's probably phoned half of Tuckers Bluff by now."

"Ain't that the truth," Ruth Ann sputtered through laughter. "If he hasn't called every breathing resident by now, there ain't a cow in Texas."

The women all chuckled, but Nora seemed to grow more interested in the new stranger.

Aunt Eileen must have noticed Nora's interest as well and turned to Abbie. "Was he wearing a ring?"

Abbie straightened and winked at Aunt Eileen before shaking her head. "No ring. No tan line."

A sourpuss of a man walked into the place and without acknowledging Abbie's wave or any of the folks who'd looked up as he came in, the old goat slid into the booth across the table from the new talk of the town.

"Well, ain't that just like that ornery old mule." Ruth Ann shook her head. "Maybe it is a good thing he's selling that feed store and young Jake and his wife are moving back to Houston. Being around an attitude like that can't be good for a person's health."

"I wonder how Jake Sr.'s wife has put up with him all these years." Sally May set down two cards and retrieved the two new ones Nora dealt out.

"They say love is blind." Ruth Ann tossed down two cards as well and smiled at the ones dealt her.

"To be married to that man, love would have to be deaf and dumb too." Aunt Eileen tossed a chip into the pot. "I'm in."

Sally May shrugged and tossed in a chip. "I'll see you."

"Me too." Ruth Ann followed and Nora folded her cards and shook her head.

Grinning, Aunt Eileen spread her cards face up in front of her. "Three ladies."

The table groaned and Joanna laughed. If Aunt Eileen's luck had been bad earlier, the walk to the library had certainly turned it around. She'd won every hand since they'd returned to the café.

"Are you sure you don't want to play a hand or two?" Sally May shuffled the cards.

Joanna scanned her notes and looked up at Ruth Ann, shaking her head. "Thanks but I'd like to know more about your ancestor the blacksmith. The one who came to Texas after the war and married a mail order bride."

"Right," Ruth Ann smiled. "From what I remember, my grandmother had said the family had moved from Three Corners because of the school. I think she meant her mama, because most of her stories were about her growing up here in Tuckers Bluff."

"Didn't they use to use churches for schools around the turn of the century?" She scribbled *moved for school* on the page.

Ruth Ann shrugged. "Don't know. I do remember my grandmother was really proud that *her* grandmother was one of the groups of brides that had come west. Tough breed, she'd say. Survival of the fittest."

"I can't imagine what all that generation had to endure to forge a life in the Wild West." Joanna's own encounters with the native rattlers was unsettling enough. Having to carve a life with a complete stranger—how difficult was that? If she were honest, it was that very aspect that had sucked her in to writing the story. Not that she could imagine packing up and hauling herself halfway across the country on a wagon train, or even a regular steam train, to marry a total stranger, but nonetheless, there was still something incredibly romantic about the whole thing.

"If you really want to know," Ruth Ann closed her cards, "I have some of my great grandmother's journals at home. They've been passed down for years. I don't think anyone after my grandmother has taken the time to read them." She fanned her cards out again. "It would be kind of nice to have someone interested after all these years."

"Absolutely." Joanna almost sprang out of the seat and hugged the woman she'd just met. Everything was coming together so well she could hardly believe it. So many ideas churning in her mind.

At that moment, Aunt Eileen's nose crinkled. "Looks like the feed store has a new owner."

The two men across the cafe shook hands. The one in the suit pushed some papers across the table and the older man that everyone had proclaimed was as much of a grouch as he looked, scribbled at the bottom of a few pages. Without even a goodbye, he then pushed to his feet and slid out of the booth.

The man in the suit folded the pages into a larger folder, stood, tossed several bills on the table and spotting all the women looking his way as he turned, waved and nodded and flashed a smile that would have made Joanna's knees weak if she were in the market for a man. Instantly her thoughts ran back in time imagining two different brides to be, one arriving to Mr. Sourpuss and the other to Mr. Suit. No matter how she turned it over in her mind, neither scenario compared to being rescued by Finnegan Farraday.

• • • •

The entire Farraday clan took up the front pews in the quaint white shipboard church at the other end of town. Seated beside Ethan, Joanna heard the buzz of his phone in his pocket. He pulled it out, his hand poised to send it to voicemail when a frown settled between his brows. The caller ID must have caught his attention. Leaning over, he whispered to his father, "I need to take this. It's Brooklyn."

All the faces within earshot turned to Ethan and several pairs of eyes followed him down the side aisle and out the back door. Aunt Eileen glared at the front row as if they were a line of children and immediately all eyes returned to the front, only occasionally daring to cast a furtive glance behind them in search of their sibling. Joanna didn't have a clue what was going on, but no one had to tell her whatever that call was about, it was something serious enough to have dropped a heavy blanket of tension over the entire family.

With no sign of Ethan returning, when the service came to an end, the Farraday clan shot up and made it to the rear of the church and out the back door.

Ethan's voice carried from the side path along with his footsteps. "Got it, man. Thanks."

The group of siblings and loved ones circled around giving Ethan the illusion of privacy. A few admired the flowers, a couple more studied the architecture, but when it was clear the conversation was over, Mr. Farraday was the first to speak up. "Anything we should know about?"

Ethan looked from the phone in his hand to his father. "I honestly don't know."

"Well," Aunt Eileen gave up any pretense being interested in the recent paint job the church had undergone. "What exactly did he say?"

"He wanted to know if Francine sings?"

"Sings? What kind of a question is that?" Finn's dad asked.

Ethan faced the family gathered in the open courtyard. "Francine's social security number popped up on an auto search. Either Francine, or someone using her social security number, has been hired on by Towing the Line."

"Is that a band or a junkyard?" one of the women asked.

Gripping the phone tightly, Ethan's hand fell to his side. "From what Brooklyn has uncovered they're a country music band and Francine is their new member. A backup singer. He's sending someone to Nashville to see if it's really her."

"Do you know?" Aunt Eileen asked. "If she can sing, I mean?"

Ethan shrugged. "No. I don't remember her humming or anything. What little I know, her dream was to be an actress."

"When will he get back to you?" his father asked.

"Soon as he knows something new." Ethan tapped at his phone. "Until then, I'm going to check in with Allison. Maybe she can give us an idea if this is really Francine or someone is just using her ID."

“And if it’s her,” their father asked, “what are you going to do?”

Phone to his ear, Ethan stepped back toward the church. “Damned if I know.”

CHAPTER FIFTEEN

Finn stood with his family staring at his brother's back as he headed into the auxiliary building where the infant care and child classes were held. No one moved. The odd call had come as a bit of a surprise for him, and from the sounds of silence, everyone else as well. He certainly knew he hadn't expected news of Brittany's mom anytime soon.

"Does it matter?" Connor asked the family, but looked at his wife.

Catherine shook her head. "Not really. The judge revoked her parental rights. Ethan has full custody. If Francine doesn't reach out to him, he doesn't have to reach out to her. Even if she does reach out, he doesn't legally need to respond."

All his brothers exchanged a look. They knew Ethan. For him, for any of the siblings, legal requirements and the right thing to do might not be the same thing. Though the entire family knew for dang sure that there was no way Ethan and Allison would ever legally restore Francine's parental rights, they also knew Ethan would never stop her from visiting with or knowing about her daughter.

Finn noticed Joanna standing quietly to the side, a little stiff, taking in the conversations and concerns, doing her best to melt into the scenery. It was almost funny, but no one seemed to be responding to each other as though a near stranger were in on the private discussion. It was as if she were another member of the family. A recent addition like Catherine or Meg, or Toni. Even though Becky had always been like family, her part in the conversation was more due to the fact that very shortly she would *be* family. Only Joanna wasn't anything close to family.

Aunt Eileen tapped Finn's dad on the arm. "No point standing here growing roots. It's probably nothing." She turned to Finn. "You going to see the sisters?"

Finn nodded and inched closer to Joanna. "We'll be home in time for supper."

"Good."

"We might be a little late." Meg hooked her hand through her husband's elbow. "I have a last minute guest checking in and I don't know exactly what time he's arriving."

"Make it when you can," Aunt Eileen smiled. "Supper's always warm in our kitchen."

One by one, everyone moved forward and dispersed in separate directions, knowing in a short while they'd all be gathering together again.

"Your family is amazing." Joanna followed him to his truck.

"They have their moments."

"More than one I'd say." She came to a halt at the passenger side. When Finn held the door for her she looked up. "You're pretty amazing too, Finnegan Farraday."

"Back at you, JoJo. Back at you." And damn if that wasn't the absolute truth.

• • • •

Sometimes Joanna had to pinch herself and make sure she hadn't landed in a fairytale. The Farradays were the personification of blood is thicker than water. Probably every person's dream family. Not that she'd had come from a bad one. One mother, one father, one sister, one dog and a two car garage in a large suburban city. Simple, statistical, and amazingly normal. No drama, no feuds, no angst. But they weren't the Cartwrights or the Farradays, either.

Finn held the car door open for her. "You look awfully serious for someone who has been bubbling with excitement most of the morning."

"Thanks. I guess I just felt really awkward being in the middle of Ethan's business."

"Don't. None of his relationship, or lack of relationship, with Brittany's mom is a secret." Finn circled around the hood and slid into the driver seat. "But I will say up until a few seconds ago when you lost that glint of excitement over going to the sisters', this writing career seems to make you much happier than what I remember from the last time I saw you."

Joanna had to think a minute. "Caitlin's wedding."

"Yep." Finn nodded.

"August. We'd barely gotten our caps and gowns and they were planning another walk down another aisle." It had been an interesting wedding. In far East Texas, with kegs of beer and lots of cowboy boots even on the women. Joanna had been surprised to see Finn there. "You were best man."

"Last minute stand in. Gary's brother broke his leg so I got promoted."

"Do you still talk to them?"

"I get Christmas cards every year. Does that count?"

"Me too, and yes it does. I keep up with them on social media too. They seem to be having fun, but even though we all swore time and distance wouldn't get between us, the singles seem to stay in touch with the singles, the marrieds with the married."

"I don't have time to play around on the computer, but I still get a call every once in a while from some of the guys. Phil Downing just had a baby."

"I didn't even know he'd gotten married."

"Someone he met at work. I guess they've been married for three or four years coming up this fall."

"Did you go to the wedding?"

"No. Wanted to but calving season is never an ideal time to take off for a long weekend in Louisiana."

"Aren't farm animals born in the spring?" Finn rolled his eyes and she realized her mistake right away. "I mean ranch animals?"

His eyes did that amused twinkle thing that always made her want to smile back. "We have both spring and fall calves on the ranch. Makes good business sense."

"Is that one of the many things you wanted to change after school?"

"One of 'em." The amusement in his eyes shifted to something more akin to satisfaction, or maybe pride.

She loved how that triumphant grin made his eyes shine. "It's nice seeing your life turn out the way you wanted."

"It's nice seeing you loving what you're doing too." His eyes twinkled even brighter and her heart went a little soft.

"Truthfully, I'm going to have to figure out a way to make this pay a little better."

"Maybe that Great American novel?" he suggested earnestly.

"I wish." If he only knew how many first drafts of total crap she'd tossed out. "It's not as easy as it sounds."

"Doesn't sound easy to me at all."

God she loved how he believed in her. Always had. "Regardless," she drew her thoughts back to the conversation at hand, "I seriously need to figure something out if I ever want a place of my own. I love living with my sister but sharing a rented apartment can't go on forever."

"Why not?"

"What do you mean why not?"

"There has to be plenty of sisters who stay together if their lives don't force them apart."

"Finnegan Farraday, if you're going to use the sisters as an example of my sister and me you had better think twice." Visions of herself and Sister with hair teased as high as it was wide was as horrifying as it was hilarious.

"There could be worse things."

"Like what?"

"One of you could lose the other."

She knew he was referring to his mom and Aunt Eileen, but the thought of losing her sister, even though she could be a neurotic nuisance from time to time, made Joanna's blood run cold. "I don't even want to go there."

"No. No, you don't."

She wondered now how much of Finn's quiet side was due to what happened to his mom. "Did your aunt always live with you guys? I mean, before your mom?"

Finn shook his head. "No. She didn't know a blessed thing about ranches. She and my mom were very close growing up and she came to visit often, but she was a city girl."

"Really? I wouldn't have guessed." She'd just assumed his mom and aunt had both grown up nearby as well.

"I was young when she came to live with us so all I remember is a very capable woman, but Adam and Brooks have some funny stories about her and the cows."

"I'd like to hear them sometime."

"Going to write a book about it?"

Joanna shrugged. "Who knows. But I'd better get through this project first."

"Depending on how long this story keeps you here, we can fill you up with all sorts of stories. And if we plow Aunt Eileen with enough of Toni's booze balls, we might even get her to sing for you."

"She sings?"

"Only at weddings and baptisms if there's enough champagne. But yeah, she sings."

Before Joanna could ask anymore about the aunt, Finn was pulling into a space in front of a cute little pastel cottage with Victorian white trim and flower covered trellises. "This is where the sisters live?"

Finn nodded. "And it looks just as frilly inside."

"Frilly. Such a good word." She'd barely had a chance to get one foot out of the truck when both sisters came running down the front flower edged path. The small swatch of front yard would easily fit into any English or botanical garden.

"We hurried home to get here before you. Poor Father Tim must have thought our shoes were on fire the way we ran out."

"Sister and I have got so much to show you. We could hardly wait. And there's still one more box we didn't have time to go through."

"Yes, but we have a nice pitcher of fresh sweet tea waiting."

"And Sister baked a chocolate chess pie."

"My grandmother's recipe."

On either side of her, the two sisters practically whisked Joanna into the house. As almost an afterthought, they called over their shoulders to Finn. "We made plenty for you too, Finn dear."

"Thank you, Miss Sissy."

Stepping inside the sisters' eccentric world, Joanna thought she might understand just how Dorothy felt when her house landed in Oz.

CHAPTER SIXTEEN

Finn had expected a long, quiet, and boring afternoon. He had not expected to get caught up in the sisters' stories and photographs. The two women had gathered all sorts of things, from newspaper articles to delicately crocheted baby shoes. The piles of family treasures made Finn want to go rummaging through the boxes and trunks he knew were in his own attic and see what kind of history he could drum up for the Farradays.

All sorts of photographs and letters were sprawled out around the table. Finn held a paper flyer that had originally brought the sisters' ancestors to Three Corners. "This is amazing." Faded and yellowed, the page was hard to read where it had been creased over a hundred years ago, but the big bold words *Brides Wanted* had his full attention.

"This here is a photo of our great great granny's sister. The one who married a miner and moved on to California."

Finn peered over Joanna's shoulder.

"This," Sissy said, "is our great great granny Lilibeth with our great grandmother Emma. According to the writing on the back, Emma was five years old."

The tan and white photo taken on a typical Victorian sofa in a surprisingly lovely home for dusty turn of the century West Texas revealed an adorable golden haired child looking every bit the porcelain doll.

"So pretty." Joanna carefully picked up a birth certificate. "Emma Elizabeth, born to Lilibeth Anne and Herman Mueller." Setting the paper down, she lifted another in the same stack. "Oh dear."

"What?" Finn set his hands on her shoulders.

"Herman died two years later."

"Yes." Sissy tightened her mouth and shook her head.

"So sad," Sister agreed. "People died young in those days from the most ridiculous things. We get the flu now and we take some sort of aspirin for the fever and drink lots of fluids. A hundred years ago people died."

"Several more letters and articles of clothing, including a picture of Emma Mueller in front of the Tuckers Bluff church on her wedding day, had been shared and studied when Finn realized that he'd kept his hands resting on Joanna's shoulders. Even more surprising was the discovery that along the trip down memory lane he'd begun to gently massage the tight muscles as well. The simple gesture had felt so natural, so comfortable, neither of them had reacted. Now, he considered pulling back, but the tension in her neck was slipping away bit by bit with every stroke.

"So your great great granny lived in Three Corners, and your great granny Emma was the first to move to Tuckers Bluff, but that was before Three Corners became a ghost town."

"I would think so. I remember my granny telling us stories about her granny coming to visit every year at Christmas when she was a little girl."

Joanna nodded and Finn felt her shoulders tighten under his fingers once again. She was probably thinking the same thing he was. All these papers and pictures and she was no closer to figuring out what caused the demise of Three Corners than she had been before.

• • • •

"I don't mean to sound ungrateful." Joanna shifted in the front seat of Finn's truck. "I had just expected fewer loose ends. I know their ancestor came as a mail order bride. Her husband died when their daughter was two years old. The daughter married a man from Tuckers Bluff and the great great grandmother stayed in Three Corners."

"That is more than we knew before you started. And they did

give us the other box to go through."

"The box had Lilibeth's name on it. Anything she has would be decades before the town came to its demise." Joanna didn't lean toward pessimism, but in this case she was just being practical. "I am simply going to have to read this journal Ruth Ann gave me before church a little faster if I want to find the reason Three Corners died."

"Is it that important to know the why?" Finn pulled away from the sisters' home and turned the truck away from town. "I mean, how big an article are you expected to write?"

"It doesn't have to be long, but with a photo spread to go with it and main cover promo, I'd like it to be knock your socks off, power packed reading."

"Any news on when the photographer is coming?" Finn asked.

Joanna shook her head. As much as she was enjoying her stay, she didn't want to become like Mark Twain's fish and wear out her welcome.

"Didn't your editor say she was in a hurry?"

"In the book and magazine business a hurry isn't quite the same as what it means to the rest of us. If an author turns in a book, it won't hit the shelves for twelve to eighteen months. Not quite a year, but still, magazines have months of work before to do before an issue appears on newsstands. Denise's *right away* and my version of right away could be weeks if not months apart."

The words "I see" had hardly left Finn's lips when Joanna's phone dinged. Glancing down, she chuckled. "Her ears must have been ringing." Placing the phone on speaker, Joanna spoke into the phone. "We were just talking about you." In the writing biz there was no such things as weekends off. When Joanna needed something handled, that was a great thing. On the other hand, when she wanted to put her work away for a short while, not so much.

"I've only got a minute, it's my daughter's birthday party today and my mother-in-law already has me searching for the corkscrew."

"Ooh. Sorry."

"Her son's worth it." Joanna could hear the appreciation in her editor's voice. "Anyhow, the photographer should be hitting your town today or tomorrow. I know he's not your favorite but on short notice it was the best I could do."

"What do you mean—"

A dog barked, a crash rang out and what sounded like a house alarm blared in the background. "Shit. I have to go. Can't wait to—" Another crash sounded. "Damn it. Bye!"

"What was that all about?" Finn stepped in closer.

Joanna was still looking at her phone, debating if she should call someone or wait. "I hope her house isn't burning down. Or worse." She slipped the phone into her pocket. "I'll give her a bit to settle things. If she doesn't check in with me soon, I'll call her back."

"Good plan."

By the time they'd made it to the ranch the place was bustling. Pots and pans were moving about, dishes were carried from room to room and everyone seemed to know exactly where to go and what to do like cogs in an insane mechanical wheel.

"I'll set this box in your room," Finn whispered in her ear and Joanna nodded.

"Just in time." Aunt Eileen looked up at Finn walking to her room with the remaining items given to them by the sisters, then turned to Joanna. "Go on and take a seat in the dining room. Finn, don't dawdle." She smacked Adam's hand as an extended finger made its way toward a large bowl of mashed potatoes. "As a matter of fact. Everyone not carrying a plate. Out."

It had been a long time since Joanna had sat down to family meal like this. Even at her parents' on Thanksgiving when aunts and uncles came over, they still didn't take up as much space as the Farradays. Joanna had met most of the family over the last few days and sat with them again this morning at church, but somehow having everyone confined around the table in one room at the same time seemed more like a class reunion than Sunday supper. From what she could gather, the only one missing was Ethan's girlfriend, the one he'd called after church. Though the talk at the table made it pretty clear that he was on a strict timeline to get a ring on her finger and make it official. Most of the hoopla was about the upcoming wedding for Becky and DJ.

"You have to have a ring bearer," Aunt Eileen insisted. "It doesn't have to be a member of the family."

"Aunt Eileen." DJ reached over and squeezed his fiancée's hand beside him. "Stacey as flower girl is all we need."

"And she will be beautiful, but she needs a little young man beside her."

"Don't you think Stacey's a little young for matchmaking?" Sean Farraday asked his sister-in-law.

"Don't be silly." Aunt Eileen shook her head. "Of course she is."

Catherine, Stacey's mom, wiped her forehead dramatically. "Whew. I'm not ready to be a grandmother yet."

The table erupted laughing and Aunt Eileen, shaking her head, joined in on the good-natured ribbing. "You can laugh all you want, but once upon a time arranged marriages worked out pretty good. Didn't they, Joanna?"

This time all heads turned to her. A few sets of eyes glanced to Finn and then back.

"Don't look at me," Finn said with his hand on his chest. Then raised it at his side. "I'm just the coc—excuse me, leech repellant."

Aunt Eileen's brows folded into a near scowl. "You were what?"

"Nothing," Finn looked to Joanna and she felt the warmth of his gaze clear to her toes.

"I think there's a story here." Adam tossed his napkin on the table. "Spill."

Meg gently jabbed her husband in the side and shook her head at him.

A couple of the brothers cracked up laughing and the dirty look Adam shot back at his siblings almost had Joanna laughing out loud too.

"There's nothing to tell," Finn said.

Joanna felt his gaze on her again and decided she'd better change the subject or pretty soon she was going to be turning bright red. "I think your aunt is referring to Ruth Ann's great grandmother's diary."

"Well, as a matter of fact, I was." Though the aunt had backed her up, the hint of a frown still resting between her brows told Joanna that the older woman might have a few questions of her own.

"Since Ruth Ann only gave me the diary this morning before church, I've only been able to skim a few pages. Mostly her ancestor's anticipation of a new life. From some of the dreams, I don't think the brides were even slightly prepared for how much harder life would be here in the West compared to the cities back East."

"I can't imagine." Catherine shook her head. "I had enough trouble getting used to the horses and the cows and I have a nice big house with indoor plumbing and a microwave and central heat and air."

"Tell me about it," Meg agreed. "Scary thought, crossing the country to marry a stranger."

"I'm sure it didn't wind up very well for a lot of women, but I skimmed ahead to the brides first meeting of the men and the way Ruth Ann's ancestor's gaze immediately drifted to the blacksmith. So it looks like it was love at first sight."

"Know how that goes," one of the brothers mumbled and another few nodded.

"Who's ready for dessert?" Aunt Eileen stood. " Apfelstrudel."

"I love that strudel." Meg grabbed a plate and stood. "Even if my hips don't."

Plate in hand, Catherine followed after Meg to the kitchen.

"My hips and I haven't been on speaking terms since puberty."

More chairs scraped against the hardwood floors, voices rang out cheerfully praising a favorite dessert and teasing how no one was quite sure how a handwritten German strudel recipe had been passed down through the generations as they worked their way into the kitchen.

"Now what?" Joanna pushed to her feet.

Hand at her lower back, Finn ushered her out of the huge dining room toward the living room where Ethan stood to one side on the phone. "You wait here. Guests don't cut their own strudel."

Dropping his phone into his shirt pocket, Ethan looked up at the two quietly entering the room.

"Looks like Aunt Eileen is dishing out dessert."

Finn nodded. "Finally get a hold of Allison?"

"Yeah. She had her phone turned off while she was in meetings all day. Let me tell you, these mucky mucks in medicine are worse than generals in the Marines. They don't believe in a day off either."

"Anything on Francine?" Finn moved closer to his brother.

"Not really." Ethan shook his head. "Allison says her sister had a beautiful voice but never mentioned anything about singing professionally. As a teen she'd always talked of acting and Allison assumed that's how Francine wound up in LA."

"Not much of a leap from acting to singing. Lots of people do both."

"Yeah." Ethan looked to the next room where his daughter Brittany was being happily passed from smiling relative to relative. "I guess." He looked back to Finn and offered a tired smile. "I'd better go retrieve my daughter and get some strudel before it's all gone. You two enjoy the quiet while it lasts." Then his grin grew wide and sincere. "Well, not too much."

CHAPTER SEVENTEEN

Memories came flooding back of Finn's older brothers teasing the crap out of him when he hit puberty and took his first serious interest in girls. Subtlety was not a Farraday trait. "Make yourself comfortable." He waved Joanna over to the sofa. "Dessert coming up."

"No need." Becky came in with two plates and holding one out to each of them. "Saved you a trip."

Joanna shook her head. "Thank you, but you didn't have to do that. I'm sure I can—"

Carrying two more plates, DJ sauntered in behind his fiancée. "Like she said, no need. Guests are guests."

Joanna's face tipped into a smile as she accepted the proffered dish and turned to sit in the nearby easy chair just as Becky slid into the spot. Before Joanna could shift to the other chair, DJ sat. In only a few seconds the family had descended into the room dragging extra chairs around to accommodate the crowd and still somehow, two spots on the sofa remained empty.

Finn recognized a set up when he saw it, but the look on his aunt's face when she walked into the room and noticed the arrangements told him this time she wasn't at the helm. To make life easier on everyone, he kicked over an ottoman and dropped down, eager to dig into the strudel.

His aunt took the spot on the sofa and Joanna sat beside her. For a few minutes the room was silent except for the sound of scraping forks against the plates.

"I can't believe what a hard time you're having finding more history on Three Corners." Adam set his empty plate on the coffee table. "I'd have thought in this day and age every resident's records would be up to date including their blood type."

"Nope." Joanna blew out a frustrated sigh. "Not even any census reports."

"I seem to remember something about a fort out that way." Finn's dad squinted up at the sky. "I was a teenager. We'd had a good old-fashioned Irish wake for my grandfather. The ranch was a madhouse the whole weekend. I didn't realize how much liquor an Irishman could hold until that day."

"And your point?" Aunt Eileen gave him one of those straighten-up glares.

"Yes. Well, after they were good and happy, Dad and Uncle George got to talking about how things had changed from Granddad's time. I remember getting the impression that things were busier when Granddad was a boy because of a nearby military base that had once been a fort and by the time my father was born had been shut down." Sean shrugged. "Maybe it's not important but if it is nearby perhaps some of the records from the base might be of help in your history search."

"That's a great idea." Joanna lit up. "I'll get on it later tonight."

"Why wait?" Empty plate in hand, Finn stood up. "Might as well start now. I'll show you to the office."

She squinted her eyes at him and did that little shift of her mouth instead of shaking her head no. "It can wait until later. We're all still eating."

"Oh, we don't stand on ceremony here. Go on," Aunt Eileen encouraged. "It's obvious you love what you do. Go do it."

Joanna glanced over at him and he could see in her eyes she was anxious to try looking up a new lead, but hesitant to leave the family gathering.

"Come on." Finn stuck his hand out at her and ignored the way all the eyes in the room casually shifted to watch her take hold of his.

"If you're sure." Joanna looked to Aunt Eileen and his dad. Both nodded. "Okay, hubby, lead the way."

At least nine heads turned to Finn as utter and complete

silence rained down on the living room.

"It's a joke." Finn rolled his eyes. "We've been over this. Remember, leech repellent?"

"Actually," Aunt Eileen's back stiffened, "you never really did explain that."

Finn blew out a sigh. "I'll explain later."

"Hmm," Aunt Eileen mumbled quietly. Adam raised a single brow. Brooks shook his head. Connor kissed his wife's cheek. Declan chuckled and turned away and then everyone slowly returned to business as usual. Though Finn had the uneasy feeling that this wasn't the end of the long running joke as far as his family was concerned.

• • • •

"Sorry," Joanna whispered as they stepped into the office.

Finn shrugged "No big deal. It's not like I'd run off and get married without telling them. They know that."

How stupid had she been to joke with Finn in front of his family. Not that she thought for a minute any of them would seriously believe Finn would marry anyone without a family entourage, but still it was a dumb move on her part.

"Seriously, JoJo." Finn flicked his knuckle under her chin. "It was a joke, they'll get it."

"I guess you're right." Settled at the computer, Joanna's fingers flew across the keys with one word then another in search of the bases. This was no longer about the boost to her career, but honest curiosity about the past. "Apparently there was a big Indian problem in the late eighteen hundreds. Texas had dozens of forts plus hundreds of temporary camps."

"We only need to track down the physical forts. Can you tell if one was near Three Corners?"

Joanna shook her head. "Still checking. The problem is finding a map from the turn of the last century."

"Be thankful back then there was no Air Force or Navy giving you more records to plow through." Standing behind her, Finn scanned the screen over her shoulder. "At least you were able to limit your search to nineteenth century West Texas forts."

"Most seemed to have been abandoned in the late eighteen eighties." Joanna continued to peruse the pages. Squinting, she tried her best to ignore the heat of Finn standing behind her. "Looks like only a dozen or so lasted into the twentieth century. Most of those were gone by the 1920s but…well, look at this."

"I'll be." Leaning in closer, Finn's chest brushed against Joanna's back and his breath tickled her neck. "Print that. Let's find a current map. Match up the size."

For a split second her mind went blank and her senses took over. These intense reactions to his nearness made no sense. She'd stood in close quarters with Finn before, hell, they'd shared a house for two years. Resisting the urge to lean back against him, Joanna refocused on the screen and did as instructed.

Finn reached for the first sheet of paper and circled the modern day road map where the remains of Three Corners could be found, then on the next page with the old map drew a similar circle at the single crossroad. The first road traveled south to the old Fort Dickson that had lasted as the only military connection between Dallas and Fort Bliss until 1944.

Excited to see the perfect fit, Joanna spun about and almost knocked heads with Finn. Had his eyes always been such a deep shade of blue? Shaking off the distraction, she pushed her chair back. "I bet this is it. And this other road leads to Fort Worth."

"Where the west begins," Finn announced in an exaggerated deep voice before returning to his normal tone. "And the hub of the cattle business at that time. Anyone going from Fort Dickson to Fort Worth would most likely pass through Three Corners."

Joanna looked at the map and almost smacked her forehead with the obvious. "Three Corners."

Finn laughed. "More like three points, but yeah, I see the connection. Where does the third road go?"

Once again, Joanna's fingers flew across the keyboard. She'd plugged in all sorts of search words. “I’m not sure.”

“Wait.” Finn pointed at the screen. “Click on that picture.”

She read the fine print under the photo of an official looking building. *Texas West Junior Agricultural College 1868 –1940.* “Oh. Wouldn’t that be interesting.” Sure enough. The west road cut through the old agricultural college.

“It’s starting to make sense. The town was founded where the three corners to three popular locations intersected.” Finn pushed away from the desk. “Very good, Miss Gaines.”

She batted her lashes and dipped her chin in an exaggerated coy southern move, “Why, thank you, Mr. Farraday.”

“And look at this.” Finn pointed to another image nearby.

Joanna zoomed in on an advertisement similar to the one she’d photographed at the library and read the small print. “Transportation now provided twice a day to Sadieville.” She moved the cursor to the bottom corner. “Nineteen twenty-one. “

“Ford’s horseless carriages made moving around Texas much easier for some folks.” Finn scanned the screen then tapped on the corner image. “Looks like this might have been the nearest town to the college.”

“I’ll have to make a trip back to the library. Maybe I have the beginnings of a second article.”

“A series?” Finn shrugged, his smile displaying an air of approval.

“Knock knock.” Becky wrapped on the doorframe. “Sorry to interrupt, but you have a visitor, Joanna.”

“I do?” She looked to Finn, though he had no reason to know anything more than she did.

Becky nodded. “I think it’s the photographer that your editor sent. He’s chatting with Meg. Seems when he checked in earlier today, she didn’t realize who he was.”

“What’s he doing here?” she asked, standing up and resisting the urge to reach for Finn’s hand. She didn’t need moral support, she’d gotten through the last six years without her friend. It was silly to want to him for back up now. But she did.

"He said he's been checking out the area and realized the address your editor gave him is on his way back to town. Shall I tell him you're busy?"

"No, no. I just hate to impose on your family anymore."

"Oh," Becky waved off the concern. "Aunt Eileen is having a great time with a single man in the living room. I'm not totally sure, but I think she's already got a girl in mind to set him up with."

"Ugh," Finn groaned. "For a single woman, that lady sure channels Dolly Levy."

Becky frowned at Finn. "Who?"

Finn's eyes widened and he looked as surprised as Becky looked confused. "You've never seen *Hello Dolly*?"

Becky shook her head and Finn spun around to look at Joanna. "You?"

"Hey," she cleared her throat and teasingly sang, "You're looking swell, Dolly. I can tell, Dolly," then chuckled. "What I'm more surprised is that you know who she is."

"My aunt loves musicals. All of them. So did my mother."

All the merriment in the banter slipped away when Joanna remembered his mother had named her children alphabetically because of the old musical *Seven Brides for Seven Brothers*.

"Excuse me," Becky interrupted. "Hate to break up the fun, but what do I tell the photographer?"

"Right. I'd better go rescue him from the West Texas Dolly." Joanna headed out the door and down the hall. Behind her she could hear Finn and Becky going back and forth about which was more surprising, that she'd never heard of *Hello Dolly* or that Finn thought of her so readily.

Several paces ahead of Finn, Joanna crossed into the large family room where most of the Farradays were still gathered. Immediately, her gaze fell on Aunt Eileen and the tall dark haired gentleman beside her and the hair on her arms bristled. No. Denise couldn't have done this to her. She had to be mistaken. All she could see was the man's back and part of his profile and just because he had the same build and similar profile and, oh heavens, that same annoying pitch to his voice, she couldn't be that unlucky.

"Good, you're here," Aunt Eileen said from beside the visitor.

As sure as her name was Joanna Gaines, the tall man to stand and face her was indeed the one photographer in the world she'd hoped to never see again. "Joanna, nice to see you again."

She managed to nod and squeak out a polite hello.

"It's been ages." He shifted and stepped forward in her direction.

Joanna didn't budge. She couldn't. "Yes. A long time."

"You look great. Married life obviously agrees with you."

"Uh." She didn't like the cheeky leer. Same damn look that had been a thorn in her side three years ago. Clearing her throat, she did her best to ignore the multitude of curious eyes that had just turned her way. "Thank you."

"So tell me," nose to the air, Mr. Attitude looked about the room, "which of these fortunate men is your husband?"

Damn. Just her luck he would bring *that* up. A few of the side conversations suddenly hushed and Joanna swallowed hard. "Oh, well, about that—"

Strong warm hands landed on her shoulders. Finn stood at her back. "That would be me."

CHAPTER EIGHTEEN

What little chatter there'd been in the room came to a screeching halt with Finn's announcement, accompanied by the crashing sound of a glass.

"Oops," Aunt Eileen apologized as stunned faces momentarily turned to her then back to the guest.

"Nice to meet you." The man Finn presumed to be the photographer stuck out his hand. "Nigel Wentworth."

"Finn Farraday," he responded, accepting the proffered hand and then returning his to Joanna's shoulder. The tension in her muscles was increasing exponentially with every second. All eyes in the room focused on him and Joanna. Expressions showing varying degrees of humor, surprise, or sheer confusion lingered silently. "Please," Finn pointed into the living room with his chin, "have a seat and tell us what you think of the project so far."

"I've already taken a few interesting shots. The light out here this time of year creates some fun shadows to work with. Denise didn't say much about the story idea." Nigel turned to Joanna. Finn wasn't thrilled with the way the guy's attention darted down to her cleavage before returning to her face. "What direction are you going to want me to go in?"

Finn couldn't help it, business or not he reached out and snatched Joanna's shaky hand in his and squeezed, then shot the photographer a *she's-mine* gaze that should have withered his balls with the precision of an arctic frost. The shift in attitude was slight but clear, Finn had made his point. From there the mood in the room shifted to business and Finn watched with amazement, and a bit of pride, as Joanna laid out exactly how she envisioned the articles and the photographs to work together. Even his family had been sucked into the concept, seeming to forget about the earlier bombshell.

A few cups of coffee later, and more pieces of strudel, the project was almost completely mapped out and Nigel stood at the front door ready for the drive back to town. "With the map you gave me, I'll drive out to Three Corners tomorrow and focus my shots there." The guy glanced at Finn standing behind his *wife,* hands on her shoulders and seemed to hesitate before swallowing hard and adding, "Want to tag along?"

Joanna shook her head. "I've got a lot more research to do."

"Okay." The guy shifted in place and Finn finally saw the idiot's shoulders slump, conceding Finn's win. "I'll send you what I've got so far and we'll go from there."

Joanna nodded. "Sounds good."

Like good southern hosts, Finn stood beside Joanna on the front porch, watching his brothers who lived in town and their wives climbing into their respective vehicles and Nigel preparing to follow them back to the B&B. Finn was pretty sure Joanna wouldn't have any trouble with that stuffed shirt again.

They were waving good-bye like characters on a Norman Rockwell postcard when Joanna's arm wound its way around his side and she leaned into him. "Thank you. For catching on. And playing along in front of your family."

"You're welcome." Without thinking Finn dipped down and kissed her temple. "Apparently it's a bit like riding a bike, once you know how to repel the leeches, you never forget." And he was damn glad he'd been here for this particular leech.

"Funny." Her head came to rest against his shoulder and they stood quietly as the train of taillights drove under the Farraday sign and turned onto the road back to town.

Since she showed no sign of moving, Finn remained in place. It had been a very long time since he'd done something as simple as hold a woman at his side, and even then he didn't remember it feeling quite so…nice. "So what's the story here?" He might as well get the background now before they returned inside to face his family.

"You know how it always goes. I was doing some freelance work for local papers. Got sent by one to do an interview of a homegrown celebrity returning to the fold for the annual town festival. Nothing special. Nigel was sent to take the pictures. It's normal for a photographer to shadow the journalist, but in this case the guy felt more like a lost puppy at my heel. Anyhow by the third day the puppy had morphed into an octopus with attitude, but it was hard shaking the guy, even when I explained I didn't like to mix work with pleasure."

Finn nodded, so far it seemed she'd mostly learned her lesson to just tell the guy to get lost.

"I'd actually forgotten about him when we bumped into each other at conference in Fort Worth. He'd skipped right over puppy dog and octopus and went straight to asshole. I just told him I already had a boyfriend. When he wouldn't let it lie, I might have said we were planning on a winter wedding."

"And how long ago was this?"

She sighed and took a step back to look up at him. "Fort Worth? Maybe two years. I've made a point to avoid working with him ever since. Honestly, it was pretty easy. I rarely do anything that requires me to work with a photographer. As originally planned for a back of the magazine small article, any one of the photos I took or a stock photo, would probably have been good enough."

Finn kind of wished she'd stayed close to him a little longer, but they were going to have to head back inside and face the rest of the family. As it was he was a bit surprised his phone wasn't ringing non-stop with questions from the ones on the drive back to town.

"I was going to tell him I hadn't actually gotten married when you stepped in."

"I'm glad I did."

"Me too. He would have just been all over me again."

Finn didn't doubt that for a single minute.

"With Nigel thinking I'm married, working with him tonight

was perfectly normal. Almost pleasant. He really is good at what he does."

"Sounded that way." Finn blew out a heavy breath. As long as this guy kept his eyes and hands on the camera, there wouldn't be a problem.

"Eventually I'll have to tell him the truth, or some variation of it." She flashed an impish grin. "But for now, thanks for playing along."

Finn nodded. Unlike college where playing along as her cock-blocker had been a simple task, like doing the dishes or washing the car, he had a feeling this time around he was going to really enjoy playing the role of devoted husband. He turned on his heel to follow her into the house and a different uneasy feeling set in. Getting even closer to Joanna now might be more than even he could handle.

• • • •

Joanna came through the Farraday front door first. On her heels, Finn quickly closed the door and stood to her side. The sound of the latch catching had every person in the room looking up. Ethan had baby Brittany sleeping on his shoulder, Connor had his little girl Stacey on his lap playing with finger strings, Catherine and Sean Farraday looked up from their chess game.

It was Aunt Eileen who stood near the kitchen entry arms folded, waiting. "We're listening."

"It's my fault," Joanna started.

"It's more of the same." Finn ushered Joanna into the room toward an empty seat. "I don't need to explain the obvious, Joanna is very pretty."

Every head in the room bobbed and Joanna glanced up at Finn. Somewhere deep inside she assumed Finn probably saw her as at least pretty. The same way most people perceived blondes with blue eyes as attractive people, but this was the first time she'd heard him say so out loud and she had to make an extra effort not to smile with delight.

"Guys in college were always hitting on her," Finn continued, "Some got down right obnoxious. A few times too damn friendly."

Every man in the room's gaze hardened as their jaws tightened and Joanna realized that chivalrous streak she counted on so heavily in Finn ran strong in the entire family, including their dad. Even Aunt Eileen's expression shifted from parental annoyance to parental concern.

"When *no* wasn't good enough, it was easier to simply say she had a boyfriend."

Catherine nodded. "Been there, done that."

Aunt Eileen turned to look at her niece-in-law and the stiffness in her stance eased. "I used to wear a ring on my right hand that I'd picked up at a flea market in high school. On occasion I'd have to move it to my left hand. But I never actually dragged a person into the fib."

Joanna opened her mouth to apologize again when Finn grabbed her arm and shook his head. "The point is y'all should know better than to think I might have kept something like being married from you. Not to mention, who the heck gets married and then stays away from their wife for six years?"

"You have to admit y'all are pretty comfortable with each other," Mr. Farraday added.

"Hell, we lived together for two years."

"Shared a house!" Joanna spat out quickly at the horrified look on his aunt's face. "Just shared a house."

Finn turned to her. "They know that. As many times as they came to College Station, they saw the house and how we all lived."

Joanna noticed the intense way both his aunt and his father watched the conversation and she realized what Finn hadn't, that they had probably always wondered. "We really were just friends."

Finn's head whipped around to look at his family. First to his father who nodded and then to his aunt who showed little change of expression. Finn simply shook his head. "It's late and the work starts early. I'm going to do a quick check outside and then off to bed."

"Yep." Connor set Stacey on the floor and stood up. "Same here. It's way past this one's bedtime."

Backs were slapped, hugs were passed around, and much like the round of good-byes earlier when Adam, Brooks and DJ left, mention was made of another day's work and next Sunday's supper.

"I think I'm going to look through what the sisters gave me." Joanna detoured to the kitchen for a knife, then once in her room, cut open the dust covered box that appeared to have been sealed for way longer than she'd been alive. The first thing to catch her eye was a stack of letters neatly tied in ribbon that brought a smile to her face. Love letters no doubt. Probably from Herman. Setting the stack aside, she retrieved more hand sewn and crocheted items and was surprised to uncover another book similar to the journal Ruth Ann had given her. Lifting it out, Joanna was pleasantly surprised to find it was only one of many journals. Carefully she took the first two and moved to the back porch.

During the day Farraday country seemed vast and barren, but not so in the dark of night. Under the blanket of bright stars against the velvet sky, the world seemed a peaceful, calm place. Comfortable. She felt at home. Pushing off the wooden floor with one foot, she set her rocker to swaying and looked at the first page. Lilibeth Cooper, Boston. "Wow."

"What?" Finn's voice carried from the porch steps.

"Look at this." She popped up from her seat and held up a book in each hand. "The sisters have their great great grandmother's journals and don't know it."

Finn came to a stop in front of her and smiled down at the two journals. "Looks like you're going to be overflowing in history."

She handed one to him and standing in from of him skimmed a few pages. "Herman was a cook." She flipped a page and smiled. "A baker in Germany, now he was a cook for the new hotel and Lilibeth was very proud of him." Flipping a few more pages, she closed the book. "I feel like a voyeur."

"This one covers the year her husband died." He closed the pages.

She twisted around and set her book down. "I didn't know them, but reading only the first few pages of her story, knowing they didn't have a long happily ever after makes me sad."

"It's too easy to live for tomorrow and not appreciate today." Finn looked over her shoulder into the distance, his expression slight and unreadable.

"A penny for your thoughts?" Joanna wondered if he might be thinking about his mother.

Finn shook his head. "Some thoughts aren't meant to be shared."

"Among friends anything can be shared."

"Anything?" His eyes bore into her, strong, dark, and serious.

She tried to brush off the intensity with a smile. "Of course."

"Even this?" His hands slid around her, his head dipped, and his mouth came down on hers in such slow motions she'd have sworn time had stood still until the warmth of his lips delicately pressed against hers, and then, she was sure if time hadn't stopped, she wished it would.

CHAPTER NINETEEN

He'd lost his mind. That was the only explanation for why Finn had Joanna in his arms, under his touch, pressed against him, her mouth one with his. And if this moment could never end, he would gladly forever give up his sanity.

In years past, they'd shared a pretend kiss. Mouth on mouth. Simple, sweet, only for show. And nothing like this. His hands eased down her back and came to rest on the curve of her hips. His gut tightened, momentarily robbing him of air. What was he doing?

"If you don't want your aunt to have a heart attack," his father's voice came from the kitchen door, "you may want to take that some place more private."

Joanna flew out of his arms so quickly she almost tripped over the rockers behind her.

"Oh." His dad smiled. "For the record, I wouldn't mind if you were really married. Good night."

"Oh my God." Eyes squeezed tightly closed, Joanna fell into the seat behind her. "What must he think?"

Finn wasn't sure he cared what his father thought as much as he worried what had just happened. He kissed her, that's what happened. Really kissed her. The kind of kiss that started in the moonlight and ended with breakfast. Damn. "I'm sorry."

Her fingertips rested gently on her lips and her gaze slowly shifted to meet his. Finn wasn't sure what he saw in those beautiful hazy blue eyes, but she did look as stunned as he felt.

"For what?" she asked so softly he almost couldn't make out the words.

"I, uh, shouldn't have done that." He took a step in retreat and stuck his hands in his back pockets for fear if he didn't, he might pull her into his arms again and pick up where he'd left off before his father had interrupted them.

Her hand fell from her mouth and her gaze shifted to the kitchen door and then over to the book before she picked it up and stood. "I'd better go inside and start reading. I think between the two women's journals I should have plenty of material for the mail order bride angle."

He nodded and took another step back, still overwhelmed by the need to reach out and touch her one more time. Shifting out of the way as she crossed in front of him, a sick feeling strangled his gut and fear of losing the friendship they'd had, of losing *her* rose squeezing his heart. "Joanna," he blurted out.

She stopped and turned to face him. "Yeah?"

"We're okay, right? I mean, you're not mad at me?"

A whisper of a smile crossed her lips and she shook her head. "We're good."

"Okay." He smiled, still a bit uneasy. "Good night."

"Night." She crossed the threshold into the house and Finn didn't move. He watched her back as long as he could see.

If they were good, if he hadn't screwed up, why did he still feel so damn unnerved? Scared? He crossed the short distance to the door, and standing in the kitchen looked to the dining room where they'd shared Sunday supper, over to the living room where he'd stood behind her claiming to be her husband. His eyes closed and his heart stuttered to a near stop.

The reason he felt like throwing up, whether he liked it or not, was simple. He was in love with Joanna. So now what the hell was he going to do?

• • • •

Closing the door behind her, Joanna sat on the edge of the bed and stared at the closed door. If not for the way her lips still tingled, she'd be positive she had imagined the magnificent kiss. It wasn't like she and Finn hadn't played the part before, but like actors in a show, before was just that—for show. Sweet, simple. None of the warmth, the heat, the fire that had singed her senses moments ago had been in the pretend lip locks from her college days. And certainly never before had she wanted so badly to go running to Finn's room to pick up where they were before his father had interrupted.

His father. With a groan, Joanna flung herself back on the bed. Boy had she messed everything up. At least she could be sure of one thing, Finn still wanted to be friends. Though he had a damn strange way of showing it.

Once again, her fingertips skipped over her lips. Why hadn't he ever kissed her like that in school? Because he was a boy scout. She sprang up from the bed and stripped out of her clothes. The man had always been a boy scout. Though she was the only person who he willingly played along with to deflect unwanted male attention, he was the first one to step up and help a damsel in distress or a friend in need. He probably helped little old ladies across the street when she wasn't looking.

Yanking her oversized t-shirt off the hook, she slid it on and plopped back on the bed, sitting Indian style. Finn Farraday was an honest to goodness gentleman. A kind and generous soul. The do-gooder routine that came so naturally for him was only one of the qualities she loved about him. *Loved?* Why was that word suddenly so startling? She loved a lot of people. Her mother and father and sister for starters. Her BFF since pre-school, Haley. Her cohorts in crime from A&M, Melissa and Cathy. She cried for weeks when her dog Missy died.

If she extended the list of family she loved to include cousins, aunts and uncles, the amount of love she had stored for so many would be virtually endless. She was just being overly melodramatic over a simple kiss. She and Finn were after all normal red-blooded people. There was no reason to make a mountain out of the molehill of a kiss. Like she'd said to Finn, they were good.

Unfolding her legs and twisting to grab the journal, she settled back against the pillows and skimmed the first pages, stopping to read every word when Lilibeth stepped off the stagecoach in Three Corners. Joanna hadn't realized that almost the second the brides had landed in town, the preacher was ready to marry the newly arrived ladies with their waiting grooms. It made sense. Jobs for women were few and far between in the nineteenth century. Heck, from what her grandmother said it was true for the first half of the twentieth century. Unmarried ladies remained under the protection of a father or brother until they were passed over to the protection of a husband. In the old west there would be no apartment buildings for the ladies to rent while they found respectable work. There would be only one place for them to stay—the home of their groom—and that wasn't happening without a wedding.

Thinking back to the first day she'd met Finn in class, her mind went over her first impressions and how easily the quiet young man and she had become friends. But how different would it have been if she'd had to marry Finn within hours of meeting him? Would her first feelings have been the same or, shrouded in fears and doubts, would she have shied away?

A smile tugged at her cheeks. The first moment she'd laid eyes on Finn she'd known he was a special guy. She'd have said "I do" in a heartbeat. Still would. The journal fell from her hands. Still would? Closing her eyes, she sucked in a long breath. "Joanna Gaines, you're an idiot."

Yes, she loved her friends and family and every pet she'd ever had, but the only person she'd ever been *in love with* was the one and only Finnegan Farraday. The same man who just announced all he wanted was friendship. Flinging herself against the bed hard, she snatched at the book again. A dull ache settled under her breastbone. How the heck was she supposed to write this story and walk away?

• • • •

Holding the silver framed photograph of herself and her sister on

Helen's wedding day, Eileen smiled. Of all the children, even though he was a boy and fit the Farraday mold, Finn looked the most like his mother. And the way he looked at Joanna reminded Eileen so much of the way Helen had looked at Sean. There was almost six years between the sisters, but they'd been close nonetheless. Eileen had teased her sister mercilessly over marrying a cowboy and moving to the middle of nowhere. Not that she could blame her, Sean Farraday was a breathtaking catch back then. Like his sons now, he was the complete package—smart, sweet, handsome, thoughtful, polite, strong enough to fight for the woman he loved and still gentle enough to love her better than anyone. Helen had fallen head over stilettos in love with him the first time she'd laid eyes on him, along with every one of Eileen's high school friends.

Helen and Sean had been so happy together, and Eileen was sure the same bright future was in store for Adam, Brooks, Connor and DJ, but she worried about Finn. He'd been born a wise old soul. By the time he'd hit puberty it was obvious to everyone that he was the heir to the Farraday ranch, not the older boys. Eileen knew he'd dated some in high school, but not much, and even less since returning from college and sharing the reins with his father.

Any other time and Eileen would have been thrilled with such a lovely bright girl in Finn's life, but not so much now. The girls could call her all colors of crazy they wanted to, but she knew deep down in the well of her women's intuition that the blessing of a stupid dog that no one knew much about was more important than any smile in her boy's eyes.

She set the photograph down and looked at the others displayed in front of her. They'd all grown up so well. "Oh, Helen. Am I being crazy? I sure do wish you were here." Tightening the belt on her robe she descended the stairs to the kitchen. She was being silly. Ridiculous. So what if her instincts were rarely wrong? They could be wrong this time. A warm cup of tea and a bit of yesterday's chocolate cake was the only answer she could come up with. For now.

Noticing the porch light on, Eileen filled the kettle and leaving it to boil, peeked out the nearby window. “What the…”

In a t-shirt and sweatpants, the same sleeping attire Eileen’s niece favored, Joanna sat hunched on the stoop talking to herself. Not till Eileen reached the back door did she see more clearly that Joanna was not talking to herself but reading from a book.

“This is the saddest day of my life. When Herman passed ten years ago I thought I might curl up and die with him. It was Miss Sadie who took pity on me. All those smiles and nods were my saving grace. So sad. Lilibeth rarely wrote in her journals after Herman died.”

Something moved and Eileen cupped the glass to see better.

“Wasn’t it sweet of you to come visit,” Joanna cooed. “I needed someone to talk to tonight. Keep me from being too sad myself.”

From under Joanna’s hand, a furry shadow shifted, *the* dog. Eileen sucked in a deep breath, and very slowly a smile graced her lips. Shutting off the kettle, she grinned a little wider before turning on her heel and heading back up the stairs. Who needed cake on such a pretty night?

CHAPTER TWENTY

Not having slept more than a few winks between tosses and turns, Finn was not ready for one of his aunt's hearty breakfasts. Even more so, he wasn't prepared for her especially chipper mood.

"Thought I'd make some rice pudding for dessert tonight. Sound like a good idea to you?"

His aunt knew darn well that rice pudding was one of his favorites, if not most favorite, dessert, so he had no idea why she asked if it was a good idea. "Sounds wonderful." He forced a smile.

The light shuffle of slippers across the wood floor told him that Joanna was up early this morning. From the tired smile she offered, he'd guess she hadn't gotten much more sleep than he had. Could she have been as mixed up about last night as he was? "Morning."

"Good morning," Aunt Eileen chirped so happily, Joanna's sleepy eyes widened with surprise.

Blinking her eyes back to normal size, Joanna offered a wan smile. "Good morning,"

"How'd you sleep?" Aunt Eileen asked.

"What little I slept was fine. I spent too many hours reading the journals I found in the sisters' box."

Finn buttered his toast in an effort to look like this morning was any normal morning. "Find out anything interesting?"

"Bits and pieces that don't necessarily make a lot of sense." Joanna set the book down on the table and went to the kettle. Finn watched a rather unexpected turn of events. Rather than treating Joanna as a guest the way his aunt had done since her arrival, she was going about her business, letting Joanna make her own tea.

Finn set his coffee down on the table and studied the two women. Joanna moved in the kitchen as though it had always been her home. She opened a drawer and Aunt Eileen shifted right. Aunt Eileen needed the cutting board and Joanna shifted left. She knew where the tea bags and sugar were and helped herself to the milk in the fridge. A time or two Finn thought he might have caught his aunt actually pausing to smile at Joanna. Maybe the last twenty-four hours had indeed been a dream and Finn was still in some alternate universe.

Hot tea in hand, Joanna sat at the table across from him. "Listen to this." She flipped a page and removed the bookmark. *"The sisters of the Sacred Heart will be good to my Emma. She'll grow up into a fine lady and have the life Herman and I had hoped for her."*

"Sisters of the Sacred Heart?" Aunt Eileen brought a cup of coffee to sit at the table.

"From what I can tell, Lilibeth shipped her daughter off to boarding school in Dallas about ten years after Herman died.

"Boarding school?" Finn tore at a slice of toast. "Isn't that a little odd for a small town like Three Corners? I mean, didn't only really rich people send their kids off to boarding schools?"

"That's what I thought. It's hard to put the pieces together because she only writes in the journals sporadically, like the anniversary of Herman's death, or Emma's birthday. There's never any mention of what's going on around her in any detail. For instance," Joanna moved the bookmark and flipped toward the back of the book, *"Emma's young man has sent me a lovely letter requesting my daughter's hand in marriage. My heart is full. The sisters assure me he is a good Christian soul from a solid Dallas family, though his Protestant faith is of concern to them, I can only be thankful that my baby has found a man as good as her father, the sort of man so many of my girls dream of."*

"What girls?" Finn asked.

"That's what I mean." Joanna closed the book. "There is little detail. An occasional mention of her girls but I have no idea if she remarried, had more children, or if she's a caregiver—"

"That's possible, I refer to my nephews as my boys." Aunt Eileen fingered the ancient journal. "This wasn't cheap. It's nice leather."

Joanna nodded. "That's what I was thinking. And a boarding school in Dallas, even if it was run by Catholic nuns, could not have been cheap either."

"How many more journals are there?" Finn did his best to focus on her story. What he really wanted to know was if she was planning on coming out to work with him again. They hadn't discussed it, and until last night, he hadn't realized how much he wanted her at his side.

"Not sure. Some of the books look more like ledgers. Once I'm done with this one I'm going to go back to Ruth Ann's ancestor's journals."

Finn nodded, still not willing to ask more about her plans.

Aunt Eileen twisted to face Joanna. "Are you going to do that this morning or are you going to head out and work with the men?"

Bless his aunt.

"Actually," Joanna took another quick sip of tea, "I think I'd like to take a short nap so I don't fall asleep on my feet."

Finn swallowed his last bite of scrambled eggs. "Sounds like a good idea." He pushed to his feet, taking one last swallow of coffee. "I'll see y'all at lunch." He had one foot out the door when Joanna came hurrying up beside him.

"Can I speak to you a second?"

He glanced over her shoulder to his aunt cleaning the counter. "Sure."

Joanna nudged him fully outside. "Remember you said you'd teach me to shoot?"

"I do." Though he'd sort of hoped she'd forget that idea.

"Do you think there might be time later today or tomorrow?" She glanced off to the barn and back. "I won't be here too many more days."

His heart did that stutter thing it did whenever he thought

about losing her. "After lunch will be good. We'll go out behind the barn."

Her face lit up like a little girl with a new pony. She flung her arms around his neck, mumbled thank you and bounced away happily back inside the house.

Rooted to the floor, he had to force his feet to move away from the porch. Building new fences was the last thing he wanted to do right now. At least for the most part it was mindless work. Maybe a few hours of hard labor would help him figure out how to keep Joanna with him longer. Forever longer.

• • • •

Beyond the shadow of any doubt, Joanna was getting awfully used to these big ranch meals. She wasn't sure what had happened, or if anything had happened and it was just her imagination, but Joanna thought Aunt Eileen was being especially sweet. Until now she had thought Aunt Eileen was one of the nicest people she'd known, but today it felt as if the woman was *her* aunt.

"I figured out ages ago that there's no such thing as too much sauce in the mixture." Aunt Eileen stuck a pan in the dishwasher. "My mother used to make the driest meatloaf on the planet. I found a recipe with a can of tomato paste in the beef mix and thought, great. Then one day I didn't have any tomato paste so I opened a jar of basic spaghetti sauce, but then I had all this sauce leftover that went bad before I could use it." She shrugged. "Next time I made meatloaf I just put the whole jar in."

"And that's why your meatloaf is juicy and flavorful."

Aunt Eileen nodded. "And that's the secret."

"You ready?" Finn came out from the back porch. "We'll take the four-wheeler."

"To the other side of the barn?" she asked.

"It's farther than it looks and besides. I'd think you've had enough run-ins with the rattler family."

Oh brother, she hadn't thought of that. "Four-wheeler sounds like a great idea." She looked around the kitchen. "Do I need to bring anything?"

"Nope. We're all set."

"Here." Aunt Eileen handed Finn a covered basket. "A little snack in case you get hungry."

Finn kissed his aunt on the temple. "You're too good to me."

"I know." She grinned up at him and then over to Joanna. "What can I say? I'm a pushover."

Finn opened the door and waved outdoors.

"Lead the way, hu...master." She'd almost let the old nickname slip. That was one habit she was going to have to learn to break fast. If she hoped to see Finn more often than every six years, she'd have to let go of old habits that made for awkward moments. Not to mention impossible dreams.

The ride to the quiet side of the barn wasn't long at all. If not for the snakes, she could have done it no problem. Finn hopped out first and standing at the side, rummaged through a bag. Pulling out a set of headphones, he handed them over to her. "I'll run through a little fast instruction. When we start shooting you're going to need to wear these. "

"Headphones?" She turned it around in her hands. "Will there be music too?"

"Ha ha. They're ear protectors. You'll be using a smaller twenty-two caliber revolver but after a few shots your ears will be ringing for hours."

"Oh." Her city girl was showing. Deep down she'd hoped, like with fixing the fences, that she'd have a chance to show Finn how useful she could be on the ranch. "What about you?"

He pulled out another pair and smiled. "Me too." Next he retrieved a gun that reminded her of an old west revolver from TV, except this one's barrel looked a little longer than what she would have expected.

"This," he held the gun out, "is not loaded." She watched carefully as he rolled the cylinder looking thing that she knew held the bullet, away from the base of the gun, then slid his finger in.

"When you're loading a gun, you always do it like this so the cylinder doesn't slide back in and accidentally discharge. The last thing you want is to shoot your foot off."

"No. I like shoes too much."

Finn chuckled and shook his head. He proceeded to explain all the safety precautions and how-tos of the weapon then placed it in her hand. "You'll want to hold it like this. Unlike TV or the movies where both hands are on the grip, you'll want to have your left hand under your right for stability."

Carefully wrapping her fingers around the handle, she rested her right hand on the palm of her left. "Like this?"

"Exactly like that." He smiled. "Now see that oil can over there?"

An oil can rested on a long bench halfway between her and the barn. "When did you set that up?"

"Before lunch." He grinned. "I had a few minutes."

Lord, how she loved this man. And blast, how she wished this was easier.

"All right. Remember what I said about squeezing the trigger. Use the sites at the end to aim for the can, and shoot."

Joanna wasn't sure she could tell the difference between gently squeezing the trigger and just pulling it, but she did her best. When nothing happened and the can didn't move, she frowned, slipped the headphones back. "This isn't going to be easy, is it?"

"You'll get the hang of it. Two things though."

She nodded, and held her arms and the gun straight out in front of her.

"One. Put your tongue back in your mouth."

"My tongue is in my mouth."

"It is now, but it wasn't before."

Raising her hand as though she were going to aim and shoot, she sited the can and heard Finn chuckle. Sure enough her tongue stuck out of the side of her mouth like a tired bulldog. "All right my tongue may have been out. But it helps me aim. I think."

"I promise you there is absolutely no connection with your

tongue and your aim. Besides, there's not any real kick to a twenty-two, but if you grow into a large gun that does have a kick to it when you fire, you could bite your tongue off."

That was an unpleasant thought. "Got it. What was the other thing?"

"Don't close your eye."

"Okay." She carefully lowered the gun at her side and turned to face him. "My eyes were not closed. I can't possibly aim with my eyes closed."

Shaking his head, Finn chuckled again. "Not eyes. Eye. One."

Again she went through the motions of aiming and again, he was right. Her tongue came out to her right and her left eye shut at the same time. "Grr," she groaned. "Let's try again."

Settling the protective gear over his ears again, Finn stood behind her as she fired at the small can. She emptied the chamber, then lowered the gun at her side and turned to her teacher. "How did I do?"

"Let's take a look." Finn trotted over to the can and back with a big grin on his face. "Not bad."

It took a second for Joanna to see the holes. She counted three and squealed. "Did I do that?"

"Yes you did."

"That's good? Right?"

Still grinning like a cat with a full tummy of cream, Finn nodded. "You know that expression, can't hit the broadside of a barn?"

Joanna nodded.

"It's true. There are people who can't aim to save their lives. You did great. Want to do it again?"

Joanna bobbed her head and waited for Finn to reset the can before loading the gun under his supervision. All set, they readjusted the earphones, she lifted the weapon, took a second to bite down on her teeth so she wouldn't stick out her tongue, but struggled keeping both eyes open to aim. "Keeping my eyes open is going to be harder than hitting the can."

“You can do it, beautiful.”

Good thing her tongue was securely in her mouth or she might have bitten it off. First he tells his aunt that she’s pretty and now he calls her beautiful. A girl could too easily get use to this. All of this. The simpler life, the great outdoors, the family all around, and of course, she smiled, shooting guns.

She fired once, took aim, twice, and again and again until the cylinder was empty. Finn trotted over and back and this time presented her with a can with five new holes. So excited, she threw her arms around his neck and squealed in his ear before letting go and stepping back quickly when she realized what she’d done.

Instead of finding Finn quiet and in awkward mode like last night, he was relaxed and smiling at her. “Looks like I’ve got another Annie Oakley.”

“I have no idea who she is, but if she can shoot, absolutely.”

His grin grew wider as his head bobbed. “She can shoot.”

“Can we go again?”

Finn laughed out right. “I’ve created a monster.” Without another word he set the target up and stood behind her. If it meant keeping him close, Joanna could stand out here shooting guns until Texas ran out of cows.

CHAPTER TWENTY-ONE

Trees were not a common sight in West Texas, but every so often a lone oak or two that someone's grandmother planted survived the heat and the drought and offered a generous covering of shade. This big old oak past the barn was one of Finn's favorites. As kids they'd climbed it, swung from it, jumped from it and as older and wiser teens had cooled off under it, picnicked under it, and napped under it. Today Finn was grateful his aunt had insisted on a blanket and afternoon snack.

Stocked with fruit and cheese and crackers and chilled lemonade, they'd taken a break from shooting practice. He hadn't expected Joanna to be so enthusiastic about it. She'd done well, but pushed to do better. What should have been just a short while of lessons and practice had turned into almost two hours and the last round, every single bullet had found the can.

"Your aunt really is an amazing woman." Joanna popped a grape in her mouth.

"You won't get any argument from me."

"I'm glad she thought of the basket. I didn't realize how much the sun zaps your strength."

"Which is why we start working cattle before sun up. It's just too dang hot to deal with them in the middle of the day." Cows apparently felt the same way, often huddling under a single shade tree or lean to.

"What can I shoot at now?"

Finn chuckled. "You've already shot the hell out of three oil cans. Don't you think that's enough for one day?"

"But my gun is loaded again." Joanna picked at a slice of cheese, looking coyly at him through those long thick lashes. "And it's not safe to keep a loaded gun around."

Shaking his head, Finn smiled wide. He had no idea how anyone could say no to her. "Tell me more about your progress with the journals and when we're done eating, I'll figure out something for you to shoot at."

"Okay." Gleefully, Joanna reached for a cracker. "I've pretty much pieced together the history of the sisters' great grandmother Emma. After she married, Lilibeth gave the young couple the general store in Tuckers Bluff as a wedding gift."

Finn's fingers froze midway to his mouth with an apple slice. "She bought them a store?"

"Yep. I don't know how a baker's widow made that kind of money, but from what I could see, the Muellers were loaded."

"I wonder if it's the same store the sisters own now?"

"I don't know, but Ruth Ann's kin didn't seem to care for them much. The few times the general store came up, Emma was referred to as 'that' woman."

"A little green eyed monster maybe?"

"I don't think so. Ruth Ann's great great grandmother was Abigail and she was big on causes. Women's right to vote, prohibition. I didn't realize how scandalous the slightest thing could be. From what I can tell, Abigail would have had apoplexy if she'd known by the sixties the country would have been all about sex, drugs, and rock and roll."

"Not everyone in the sixties were hippies."

"No, but if Abigail had her way Texas would still be dry and a woman showing her ankles would be a criminal offense."

"Wonder if it's Abigail's fault Tuckers Bluff doesn't have a bar."

"I wouldn't be surprised. She lived until 1959."

Finn had been kidding, but it wouldn't be the first time a single strong person ran a town. "Did she mention anything about Three Corners?"

"Nope. But she was on a constant tirade over Sadieville."

"Where the students at the college could travel twice a day." Finn remembered.

"I took a photo of a similar ad when I was at the library."

"You did?"

Joanna pulled out her phone and scrolled through the screens. "Guess I forgot to mention it." She held out the phone. "See."

"I wonder." Finn expanded the screen for a closer look.

"Wonder what?"

"Cigarettes, whiskey and wild, wild women." He chuckled.

"What are you talking about?"

"Turn of the century version of sex, drugs, and rock and roll. This is just a shot in the dark, but I'm thinking it's possible, more like very probable, that Sadieville had a very popular," he didn't want to say whore house. He snapped as fingers as the right word came to mind. "Bordello."

• • • •

Joanna stared at him. "But everything was so polite back then."

"Yeah, well." Finn took a swig of lemonade. "If I'm right, it would explain why Ruth Ann's great whatever was not happy. Think about it, it wasn't really all that long ago that politically correct had an entirely different meaning. Before the *Brady Bunch*, parents had to sleep in separate beds on television."

"True." Joanna's mother often complained about how difficult it was to find anything suitable for families on TV nowadays. "Clarke Gable saying he didn't give a damn in 1939 almost didn't get past the censors."

"And technically prostitution has been illegal in Texas for a heck of a lot longer than that. Some places just turned a blind eye to it. And from the looks of that advertisement, Sadieville was one of those places." Finn pushed to his feet and extended his hand to Joanna to help her up. "I think the Chicken Ranch stayed in business well into the seventies.

Joanna stood beside Finn and wished she didn't have to let go of his hand. "Chicken Ranch?"

"You've never heard of the Chicken Ranch?" He looked

honestly surprised. More so than when he'd learned Becky had never heard of *Hello Dolly*.

"Can't say that I have." Joanna shook her head.

"*Best Little Whorehouse in Texas*?" he asked.

Joanna shook her head again. "Oh, wait. That was a movie."

"It was based on a true story."

"You're kidding."

"Nope." Finn bent over and gathered the remnants from their afternoon snack and placed them in the basket. "And back in the day, A&M provided regular transportation for its freshman to the ranch as standard operating procedure."

"Now you're kidding."

Finn shook his head.

"Wow." Joanna folded the cloth they'd been sitting on. "I wonder how long Sadieville lasted? Do you think it's a town, or a place like the Chicken Ranch?"

"Haven't a clue, but something tells me if it's a ghost town, I'm going to have to add another day trip to my calendar."

Clutching the folded picnic blanket against her, Joanna dropped her free hand to her waist. "I can scope out another town on my own, thank you."

"The last two times you scoped out the landscape on your own," Finn took a step closer, the humor in his eyes gone, "I found you cornered by rattlers."

"Actually," her breath hitched just a bit at the lowered tone of his voice, "I was not exactly cornered the first time."

"Joanna." Finn took another step, putting him deep in her personal space. "In a tree, in a churchyard, wherever, I don't want to see you hurt. Ever."

The burning intensity of deep blue eyes pinning her in place had all logical thought in Joanna's brain melting. Scrambling to find words, she swallowed what little saliva was still in her mouth and managed to mumble, "I can shoot them now myself."

Finn's chin dipped in a slight motion of agreement at the same time his fingertips cupped her face. "JoJo, I…care about you.

Let me share this with you?"

Joanna had no idea what *this* was, but her head moved up and down anyway as his lips inched forward in slow motion, and then, finally, heated sparks shooting warmth to every cell in her body shoved memories of last night's kiss aside and had her melting against him. All coherent thought disappeared. Letting go of the checkered cloth, her arms lifted and draped around his neck about to pull him even closer when the softness of Finn's lips eased away, dragging a regretful moan from deep inside her.

His forehead lowered, lightly touching hers. "I think," he blew in a deep breath, "I should go collect your targets and we should head back to the house."

Sucking in a strong calming breath of her own, Joanna nodded slowly. Some part of her brain still functioning knew he was right. Other parts of her didn't care about what was right.

For a few long seconds neither moved. Then a thin smile crossed his mouth and he stepped back, his grin growing wider. "Later."

Joanna watched him trot over to the makeshift bench and oil cans, her heart galloping at a winning pace for the Kentucky Derby. She had no idea what 'later' meant but she had plenty of hopes. The bench taken down and leaned against the barn, bullet ridden targets in hand, Finn walked more slowly back toward the four-wheeler and Joanna bent down, putting the remaining leftovers in the basket and picking up the blanket she'd dropped during that toe tingling kiss.

Standing upright again she noticed Finn had frozen in place. She took only one step and then the peaceful sounds of the day broke when her eyes followed the direction of his gaze. "Shit."

CHAPTER TWENTY-TWO

S*hit*. Finn stood perfectly still. His gaze shifted from the snake coiled a few feet ahead to the four-wheeler halfway between him and Joanna, then back. If he took a step in retreat he could circle around to the vehicle. Or he could take a step back and the damn snake could strike. Fully extended and biting mad, at this distance the snake could easily sink his teeth into Finn before he'd taken enough steps to clear the danger zone. *Damn.*

Not willing to make a sound, not even move his hand to alert Joanna of his predicament for fear of alerting the snake as well, Finn sucked in a deep breath and silently scolded himself. He knew damn well not to walk around the fields this time of year without a weapon handy. Even if they were in a pasture not far from the house, one that the horses grazed on keeping the grass from growing tall, snakes and West Texas went hand in hand, like peanut butter and jelly or beer and pretzels.

At this point, Finn didn't have much choice. Knowing Joanna was nearby to call for help if the snake leaped forward, he was willing to take a chance that if the stupid rattler did just that. Finn's odds were fifty-fifty that the viper would get his boots. Stepping away was Finn's only chance.

Slowly, not moving any other part of his body, Finn eased back half a step. The snake's rattle increased in volume. Or maybe that was just Finn's imagination. Taking in a calming breath, he eased back another step with his other foot, and then he saw it. What should have been a flash of speed played in his mind in slow motion. Mouth wide open, body uncoiling, the rattle snake lurched forward, and steeling himself for a nasty bite, Finn flinched as a loud shot rang out and then another.

Blinking once then twice, Finn looked down. The striking snake was not latched onto his leg or boot, but writhing on the ground at his feet. Tearing his gaze away from the threat, he managed to lift his head in time to see over one hundred pounds of Joanna Gaines fly into his arms knocking him to the ground.

"Oh my God," she cried, her hand touching his face, his neck, his chest. She squirmed shifting positions and twisted patting down each arm. "Are you all right?"

He was, but if she kept patting south he was going to be in serious trouble. "Fine."

"Are you sure?" The alarm in her eyes was both comforting and amusing.

"Nice shot," he mumbled, still catching his breath.

Joanna nibbled on one side of her lower lip and nodded. "I've never been so scared in my life. That snake is a hell of a lot smaller target than an oil can."

Finn nodded. She was right. And frankly, he was just a little surprised she'd actually hit it, but grateful as hell that she had.

"I couldn't stand the thought of you bitten. Losing you after finally finding you again." Leaning back so she was sitting on his thighs, she stretched one hand down and touched his jeans. "He didn't bite you, did he?"

Finn shook his head and sucked in a breath, then smiled. *Finally finding him again?* The words filled his chest with unexpected joy. "We really should stop meeting this way."

It took Joanna a few seconds of confusion before a smile touched her lips as well. "Not the way my Daddy did it."

Finn felt his grin tug wider across his face.

"Guess I weigh more than I did when I was six?"

Finn nodded. "You are definitely not six anymore."

"And I guess that's a good thing."

Finn's chin dipped and his arms stretched forward, tugging her fully against him. In a single swift move, he spun her around and hovered over her, energized by her squeal of delight. "What do you think we should do about it?"

Her smile took over her face and her arms linked around his neck. “I have a few ideas, hubby.”

His arms wound around her pulling her in for a kiss. *Oh, yeah.*

CHAPTER TWENTY-THREE

Joanna so was excited she could hardly contain herself. The entire drive back to the ranch from town she'd been bopping in her seat, running all the different bits of information over in her mind, fitting the pieces together like a crazy jigsaw puzzle.

For the second time this week, she'd buried her head at the library. When she'd heard from Ned that he had the afternoon free, she hurried over to sit out front and drink sweet tea. He'd been right about one thing, life took on a whole different feel when you slowed down enough to just sit and watch.

Turning under the large Farraday Arch, Joanna almost squealed, eager to share her findings with Finn. The last few days had been absolutely amazing. So little had changed between them, and yet, everything had changed.

Pulling up next to Adam's car, Joanna ran inside. "Oh. My. God. You won't believe it."

Finn was the first to meet her midway between the kitchen and the front door. "What won't I believe?"

Normally, she was rather discreet about showing her affection for Finn in front of his family, but tonight she didn't really care if the whole world was watching. She flew into his arms, wrapping her arms and legs around him. "I figured it out!"

Finn's eyes grew dark and before she knew it, she'd leaned in and planted a kiss on Finn's mouth that had her forgetting everything else except that she was finally here really with him.

"Figured what—" Meg's voice came to a stop just behind Finn. "Looks like here we go again." The sound of her heels clacking on the hard wood floor disappeared into the kitchen.

Reluctantly, Joanna slid down to stand on her own feet again and eased back a step, her brain a little rattled. Along with a few other body parts. “I, uh…”

“Figured something out?” Finn said.

“Right.” All the excitement was back. Grabbing his hand, she dragged Finn to the kitchen where a good number of the Farradays were gathered, including a new face.

An attractive dark haired woman slid out from under Ethan’s arm and reached forward, offering her hand to Joanna. “I’m Allison Monroe.”

“Nice to meet you. Joanna Gaines.”

Allison’s gaze shifted to Finn and back to Joanna. “Nice to meet you as well.”

The first thing Joanna noticed about the famous doctor was the way she immediately stepped back, tucking herself into the crook of Ethan’s shoulder. The next thing she spotted was the way Ethan stared down at her. If Joanna could bottle the way the Farraday men looked at the women they loved, she’d be richer than anyone on the planet.

“So don’t keep us hanging.” Aunt Eileen pulled a covered dish from the oven. “What’s all the excitement about?”

“Oh.” Joanna turned to find Finn at her side.

“Yes. I want to know too.” His gaze leveled with hers and her breath caught in her throat at the same sappy look she’d just seen on Ethan. “Joanna?”

She turned to face everyone. “You know I’ve been struggling putting the pieces together of what happened to Three Corners.”

A few heads bobbed as they went about their business sorting dishes and preparing for dinnertime.

“We figured out from the journals that Lilibeth Mueller was a mail order bride who lost her husband early and then took on work in Three Corners as a cook. She somehow made enough money to send her daughter to private boarding school in Dallas.”

“Must have been big tippers,” Adam teased.

Joanna laughed. “You might say that.”

“Oh.” Aunt Eileen hung up the potholders and pulled up a chair. “I think things are about to get interesting.”

"Yes." Joanna leg go of Finn's hand and sat down beside Aunt Eileen. "We knew Three Corners must have prospered because of where they were situated between three major revenue sources in the area."

A few heads nodded.

"Today I found an obituary for Sadie Chegwidden, the honorary mayor of Sadieville in 1910. She and her sister had come from the east after the Civil War and built the grand Parlor House."

"Parlor house?" Aunt Eileen repeated.

"Having learned to read between the lines, I'm pretty sure she ran the house of ill-repute that the agriculture college used to shuffle students off to."

Finn's hand fell on her shoulders. "Very good detective work."

"It gets better." Joanna covered one of his hands with hers. "After the library I stopped at Ned's for a bit."

"A bit?" Meg rolled her eyes. "Does the man even know how to have a short conversation?"

"No," Joanna and Eileen deadpanned in unison then laughed.

"After a while Ned shared a story about a camping trip he'd done as a boy with his dad and grandfather. Somewhere between the fish and wilderness stories—"

"Not the one about the catfish with teeth the size of a tiger?" Sean Farraday said with laughter in his eyes.

Joanna nodded. "That would be one of them, yes. Anyhow, in the middle of the story he mentioned his dad and grandad always took him to the ice cream shop in Sadieville on the way home. I asked if he remembered where Sadieville was." She turned to look up at Finn. "He said Three Corners."

"What?" Finn's brows buckled together. "That doesn't make sense."

Joanna wouldn't be surprised if her head fall off from nodding so hard. "But it does! In Lilibeth's journals she thanks God for Miss Sadie." Joanna looked from person to person. "Sadie. Sadieville. Lilibeth's girls."

Everyone continued to stare rather blankly.

"Oh for heaven's sake." Joanna shook her head and leaned forward some more. "After Herman died, Miss Sadie took Lilibeth in."

"Conjecture," Catherine said softly.

"That would explain the comment in the diary about thank God for Miss Sadie. And it would explain the article mentioning the new cook in Three Corners the same year Herman died—"

"Still circumstantial," Catherine added.

"I know, but the ledgers in Lilibeth's belonging begin in 1910, the year Sadie died."

Catherine leaned forward, her brow buckled in thought. "So what you're proposing is that when Sadie died, she left Lilibeth the Parlor house?"

"Yes!" Joanna smacked the table and pushed to her feet. "Lilibeth was a madam!"

• • • •

Scooping Joanna up in his arms and giving her a huge congratulatory kiss may not have been the smartest thing Finn had ever done, but it was indeed one of the most satisfactory.

"Excuse me," Adam cleared his throat. "Family watching."

"Oh yeah." Finn released his hold on Joanna. "Now you're worried about public displays of affection. You didn't sound all that concerned when we were remodeling the B&B."

Adam grinned at his wife. "That was different."

"Sure it was," Ethan teased, even though he hadn't been in Tuckers Bluff most of that time.

"Do you have anything else on it?" Finn asked.

"I do," Joanna practically squealed. He absolutely loved how excited he was about all this. "I decided to look up a few things on the agriculture college that closed down when they opened Texas Tech. Turns out that it closed only a couple of years before the old fort."

"Which means bye-bye to most of the business," Aunt Eileen added.

"Who knew we had our own little piece of Chicken Ranch like history in our midst."

"Chicken Ranch?" Catherine and Allison echoed.

"*Best Little Whorehouse in Texas*," Joanna and Finn replied, then burst into laughter.

Joanna pushed away from the table and stood. "I want to look over the journals again and see if things make more sense now that I have a better handle on the history."

"So you're going to have a good hook for your article?" Finn asked.

"This is all so much bigger than an article. I'll give Denise the piece on the mail order brides. I'll focus on Lilibeth and her sister. There are some fun letters in the box."

"Oh how nice." Aunt Eileen stood up too. "I'd better get busy. Supper will be served in a few minutes. Catherine, would you mind setting the table?"

"Not at all." She reached for the stack of plates and folks began moving around again.

Stepping out of the way, closer to the hall, Finn pulled Joanna into the circle of his arms. "What are you going to do with all this information?"

"Promise you won't laugh?" she asked.

Finn knew what was coming next. "The book?"

She bobbed her head. "I thought historical fiction."

"It will be great."

Her head tipped sideways and she seemed to study him with curiosity. "You have always believed in me."

"Always. You've never given me any reason not to."

"You're amazing." She splayed her hands on his chest between them. "I may have to bring you home with me to keep encouraging me."

"Or," he lowered his voice, "you could stay here."

He felt her suck in a deep breath and he blinked. "I mean,"

Finn reached over to his right hand and removed his Aggie ring, then lifting her left hand, slid it onto her thumb and took a deep breath of his own. "I thought maybe we could do the hubby and wife thing for real this time?"

Joanna's smile stretched across her face and her head bobbed up and down as her arms snaked around his neck. "Ab-so-lute-ly."

His mouth came down on hers and somewhere in the hazy background of oohs, aahs, and a cat whistle or two, Finn heard a muffled voice ask, "So does this mean they're going steady?" followed the smack of a hand on skin and, "It means we have another wedding to plan."

EPILOGUE

From her seat beside Becky, Grace looked up just as Joanna Gaines, soon to be Farraday, scanned the café. Spotting the two of them, she charged forward. The woman had a mission.

When Grace arranged to take time off to be in Tuckers Bluff in order to help with last minute details of her best friend and DJ's wedding, she had no idea she would soon be the last unmarried Farraday.

"Holy. Cow." Joanna fell into the seat across from Grace and Becky, leaning forward, hands flat on the table, her brand new diamond ring twinkled under the lights. "You won't believe who just called me."

"Spill," Becky said anxiously.

"Remember I signed with that literary agent my magazine editor knows?"

Becky nodded.

Grace had heard, but she hadn't been around for the details as they'd happened. She knew Joanna had made friends with pretty much everyone in town in short order. But since Finn slipped his Aggie ring onto Joanna's finger at supper not long ago, in front of God and the half the Farraday clan, as a precursor to the shiny number currently twinkling under the lights, Joanna and Becky had bonded like white on rice. As much as Grace liked Joanna and loved Becky, she felt just a teeny weensy bit left out. Her own fault for moving so far away, but she had two weeks of girl time coming up to get to know Joanna better too. She was so ready to play for a change.

"My agent sent the proposal and we've heard back already."

Becky leaned forward a bit and nodded. Grace had to admit,

that had her attention too.

"Not just one of the big five publishing houses." Joanna almost shuttered with excitement. "But three!"

"Oh that is good news." Becky grinned wide and then turned to Grace with a slight frown, then back to Joanna. "Wait, you mean three different publishers want your book?"

Joanna's head bobbed up and down so fast, Grace was afraid it might snap off. Not that she blamed her future sister-in-law. Grace wasn't a writer but even she knew how hard it was to get a publishing contract.

The bell over the café door rang and Joanna's head whipped around. The second her gaze landed on Finn, her entire expression softened.

The thing that amazed Grace was that from the moment her stoic, silent, blend-into-the-background brother laid eyes on his fiancée, his entire demeanor beamed with so much happiness if it were electricity he'd be a power house.

"Hey." Finn slid into the booth beside Joanna and leaned in for a short, sweet, simple peck on the lips.

What Grace didn't understand, since the little kiss hadn't lasted long enough to measure with a stopwatch, why did she feel as though she were intruding on a private moment? Their gazes linked a few more seconds and an entire conversation took place without words. And *that* conversation was what had made Grace feel like an interloper.

Becky tapped the table and looked at Finn. "Enough with the cow eyes."

"Yeah, you two." Grace loved her brother, but if he didn't stop staring at Joanna like she was the last frozen Popsicle in the world during a scorching August heat wave, Grace was going to heave. "We want details—about the book. And who is going to publish it."

Joanna nodded. "That's just it, I don't know yet."

Finn squeezed her hand, she shuddered again, more from the excitement than from his touch, but then again, from the way

Grace had observed these two cuddling up like lovebirds in winter, maybe Finn was the one getting Joanna's feathers all ruffled. And now Grace was feeling just a teensy weensy bit jealous again. She wasn't looking for a man of her own. Really she wasn't. She'd spent too many years in school getting her degrees and had lots of big plans for enjoying the world, but still, a small part of her would kill to have a man look at her the way Finn stared at Joanna.

"And that's not all." Joanna took in a long deep breath. "One of the houses asked how much to take it off the table."

"English please." Becky looked about as ready to jump out of her skin as Joanna was.

"Apparently, it's called a pre-empt, if we don't agree to a price the book will go to auction."

"You're kidding?" Wide eyed, Becky leaned back in her seat. "I'm going to have a famous author for a sister-in-law."

"Well, I wouldn't go that far."

"I would." Grace smiled at Joanna's bashful grin. "And as soon as it's made into a movie, I'll tag along for the red carpet walk."

"Oh, I don't think—" Joanna started.

Grace put her hand up. "Always dream big. After all, everything's—"

"Bigger in Texas," Becky and Joanna chorused with Grace and three erupted in laughter.

"It's going to be really fun having you home again for more than a long weekend," Becky said with a big smile on her face.

Finn nodded his head and the smile he flashed his sister reminded her of how much she missed her brothers some days. "Maybe Gray will show up and keep you here."

"Gray?"

Joanna looped her arm through Finn's. "That's what he calls the matchmaking dog."

"Ha." Grace practically cackled. "There's no way any dog is going to keep me here. Trust me." She knew every man in and around Tuckers Bluff. Young, old, tall, short, and there was no way under God's green earth—dog or no dog—the man of her dreams was anywhere near this dinky town.

Enjoy an excerpt from

Grace

Propping the alley door open, Chase Prescott looked left then right. No sign of his new friend. Dropping another bag onto the pile, he would have loved to shut down, remodel, upgrade, and reopen his new business, but common sense told him that in this small market he could not afford to lose even one customer to inconvenience. Within a week of signing on the dotted line, Chase had been doing his best to get in a couple of hours work cleaning out decades of worthless merchandise before opening the doors to customers each day. On only the second day he'd been putting out the trash and noticed a stealth dog lurking down the alley.

Strong intelligent eyes captured Chase's attention. Back in Manhattan, it seemed everyone he knew had small yappy dogs with polished toenails and ribbons atop their heads. Convinced this magnificent animal was foraging for food, Chase stepped inside and returned with a dish of leftover lunch only to find the dog had vanished as quickly as he'd appeared.

The following day, having drawn closer, the prowling animal paused to regard Chase as though sizing him up before moving on. This same ritual had become part of Chase's routine the last few days. Almost time to lock up, Chase wondered where was his daily visitor?

Around from behind the mountain of outdated dry goods along the alley wall, familiar amber eyes once again sized him up. "Have I not passed the test yet?" Chase crouched down on his haunches waiting to see if today would be the day the dog would finally come close enough for him to check for any signs of ownership. Patiently balancing in place, Chase resisted the urge to fist pump the air when slowly the furry canine crept up in front of him.

Scanning the dog from head to rump, he searched for signs of injury or starvation. Though the fellow looked pretty lean, Chase suspected it had more to do with a high metabolism. "Somewhere," he held his hand, palm open, for the dog to sniff, "in your family tree I'd bet there's been a wolf or two." Or three. Odd patches of color indicated his maternal ancestors had more than likely been cattle dogs. Maybe border collie. More comfortable of the animal's friendly nature, Chase raised his hand to scratch behind the dog's ears, surprised when he leaned his head into Chase's touch. "Okay, maybe I'm wrong. Maybe you do belong to someone."

The old fashioned bell over the front doors sounded. Not the obnoxious dong of modern electronics but the delicate jingle of an era long gone by. Slowly, Chase pushed to his feet. "Sorry boy, I've got to take care of business." Every time that sound rang, a shot of adrenaline spiked, propelling Chase eagerly forward. Who knew a stupid bell could be so exciting.

Four years at one of the best business schools in the country. Ten years on Wall Street making his mark on the world—and his bank account. Now the remainder of Chase's resume would be minimized to owner of a small town farm and feed store—and God how he already loved everything about this place.

The local police chief stood in the doorway with a tall man cut from the same cloth beside him. "Hey."

"Chief." Any other place and time and Chase would have assumed a visit from the local authority meant something somewhere had gone wrong. Here, he'd already learned, paying a social call was the norm.

"Finn Farraday." The chief's almost clone stuck out his hand. "Nice to meet you."

"Same here." Before agreeing to buy out the feed store, he'd done some checking around and knew the Farradays owned one of the largest ranch operations in the county. From what little information Mr. Thomas had shared after the sale, the Farradays had always been one of the stores best customers.

"I see you're not changing the name?" Finn waved a thumb over his shoulder indicating the storefront behind him.

“Not—”

“Well, look who’s here.” The Chief squatted down, and with its tail wagging, the stray trotted up to him. “Don’t you look happy.” The police chief began a two handed under the neck rubdown. Had the dog been a cat, he’d be purring.

Grinning, Finn leaned over to scratch the dog’s back then suddenly stopped, cocked his head, and squinted. “Does Gray look a little taller to you?”

Tilting his body back a bit, the police chief shook his head. “Nope.”

“You’ve got a nice dog, Chief.” Chase thought the strong lithe dog suited the man.

“Not mine.”

Chase looked to Finn.

“Nope.” Finn shrugged. “Not mine either.”

“Hm. Sure looks like he belongs to somebody.”

“That’s what we all thought.” The Chief patted the dog and stood upright. “If you figure out who he belongs to, make sure to let us know.”

Chase nodded and wondered who all was we all. “Sure thing.”

“Well,” Finn stretched out his hand again, “I just wanted to introduce myself and give you a welcome to town. I’ve been late getting around to it, but things have been a bit hectic.” He sprouted a grin even wider than when he’d spotted the dog. “Just got myself engaged.”

The pieces fell together. Staying at the B&B until he figured out housing of his own, he’d heard a good deal about the Farradays. Already having met Adam, Meg’s husband, and the police chief, it shouldn’t have been such a surprise to find the family resemblance extended to more of the siblings, but it had surprised him to realize the strapping man in front of him was the recently engaged youngest brother. “Congratulations.”

Frowning, the police chief stepped aside. “Back door open?”

Chase nodded. “Yeah, that’s how…” He looked around. “Where did he go?”

“That’s what he does.” Finn shook his head and took another step toward the rear.

The bell over the door sounded, and like a shooting star, Gray sprang up out of nowhere, bolted past the three men and galloped forward.

“Shit,” three male voices echoed.

Visions of wolf fangs sinking deep into an unsuspecting customer had Chase sprinting after the animal. Damn it. Finn on his heels, Chase saw the Chief reach for his holster and Chase’s heart skipped a beat. He didn’t want to see the dog hurt, but friendly or not, strays could turn. Just what he needed. Less than a week in town and already he would be making front-page news for all the wrong reasons.

A loud howl pierced the panicked silence. All at once a tall brunette closed the door behind her, arms stiff the chief raised his gun at the door, and the lightening quick dog leapt up knocking the lady off her feet into a display of garden seeds.

Arms and legs flailed. Packets flew left and right. The woman let out a stunned yelp and the Chief and his brother stood silently on either side of her.

“What the..?” Rather than find a bloodied victim, Chase came to a stop at the dog standing akimbo over the prone woman, licking her face.

The two brothers burst into laughter. The chief holstered his gun and Finn turned, slapped Chase on the shoulder, and muttered, “Here we go again.”.

MEET CHRIS

USA TODAY Bestselling Author of more than a dozen contemporary novels, including the award winning *Champagne Sisterhood*, Chris Keniston lives in suburban Dallas with her husband, two human children, and two canine children. Though she loves her puppies equally, she admits being especially attached to her German Shepherd rescue. After all, even dogs deserve a happily ever after.

More on Chris and her books can be found at
www.chriskeniston.com

Follow Chris on Facebook at ChrisKenistonAuthor
or on Twitter @ckenistonauthor

Questions? Comments?
I would love to hear from you.
You can reach me at chris@chriskeniston.com